OPERATION BUCKINGHAM

THE LAST TEMPLARS - BOOK 5

PRESTON WILLIAM CHILD

Edited by
ANGELA WALKER

*"Science cannot solve the ultimate mystery of nature.
And that's because in the last analysis,
we are a part of the mystery
we are trying to solve."*

~ Max Planck ~

---

*"We're not what happens to us.
We're what we do with it."*

~ Quinton "Q" Marshall ~

PROLOGUE

Retired Navy Captain Augustus Tucker Baird wore a faint smile as he lifted a bottle of Remy Martin Louis VIII cognac from the deep bottom drawer of his broad oak desk and poured two glasses for himself and his guest, who was seated in an easy chair behind him. The captain always smiled when something or someone brought his late wife, Eleanor, to mind. And that afternoon, thoughts of her were brought to mind by his guest, Father Patterson, rector of Saint Paul's Church. The fresh-faced young rector had formed a warm friendship with Eleanor in the three short years he'd served at St. Paul's before her death, and he officiated at her funeral nearly two years ago.

But the captain's smile had an added significance that Saturday afternoon. He knew how surprised and pleased Eleanor would be to see him sharing conversation—and his favorite cognac—with the rector in their home after her many failed attempts to get him to do it while she was alive. The captain's smile grew broader as he handed the rector a glass of cognac and settled into the other easy chair with a glass of his own.

"Cheers," the captain said and raised his glass with more cheer than he'd felt in months.

"To the everlasting glory of our Savior, Jesus Christ!" Father Patterson pronounced with a faint hint of a Scottish brogue, then clinked glasses with his host and took his first sip of the best cognac he'd ever tasted.

"How wonderful!" the young clergyman noted as he turned the glass slowly in the early evening light from the window and studied the elixir's warm, amber color.

Remy Martin Louis VIII, 1917," the captain said. "I keep it handy for special occasions."

"Really?" the rector replied with the look of hope in his eyes. "And why exactly do you feel *this* is a special occasion?"

"I'm not exactly sure," the captain answered honestly. "I just know that Eleanor thought the world of you and what she called your 'close relationship with God,' and she encouraged me to speak with you whenever I feel depressed. Even while she was bedridden and near death, she smiled when speaking of you and God. Shortly before she died, she made me promise that I'd speak with you if I ever felt depressed after she was gone."

"Are you feeling depressed, Captain?" the rector asked gently. "It would be totally understandable, even two years after your wife's death."

"I don't know that I'd call it 'depressed' exactly," the captain replied pensively as he glanced about the room to avoid making eye contact. "'Adrift' is probably a better word for what I'm feeling. I anticipated that I would miss Eleanor terribly, of course. But now I know that I didn't fully appreciate how large a part of my life she was. When she was here, everything about our life together was important. Now that she's gone, nothing seems important at all."

Father Patterson took another sip of his cognac and thought for a moment before sharing his thoughts.

"It seems cruelly ironic that a career naval officer who once commanded the world's most powerful war machine feels 'adrift' at this stage in life," he told the captain. "Frankly, it surprises me, given the active life you currently lead as the president's senior advisor for Strategic Military Affairs. The media made the job sound very exciting when they announced your appointment. Tensions being what they are around the world, I would guess your days—and most evenings— keep your mind occupied."

"Much of the time, it did. But the president asked for my resignation yesterday," the captain finally confided. "He wants a fresh start and new perspectives for his second term. Actually, I welcome a return to normal life, where I open my own doors and drive my own car."

"Aye," the rector said with a nod and raised his glass again. "I'm certain the White House is a rarified cocoon —but a cocoon nonetheless—and we know caterpillars can't stay in 'em forever. Here's to an equally glorious transformation."

"I welcome the change, Father," the captain said. "But still, with my job ending and Eleanor gone, I wonder if I've outlived my usefulness. I desperately wish she were still here."

"I can guarantee that you've not outlived your usefulness as far as God is concerned. And from what I can see, Eleanor is still here with you, Captain," the rector said. "From your many photos of her to her favorite books, she's everywhere I look in this house. And you must know that her spirit, the person God created her to be, never entered the grave. She's very much alive, Captain. So this separation you feel so deeply is only temporary *if* you are a believer in our Lord and Savior."

"I'm not sure I know what I believe, Father." The captain sighed and took a long sip of cognac. "Eleanor ran all that by me many times, and frankly, it all sounds like a fairy tale to me."

"Well, I assure you it's no fairy tale, Captain," the rector replied. "And I also assure you that God knows what you're going through. Don't take my word for it. Ask him for a sign—just a wink—to let you know he's with you and that he cares about what you're going through."

Father Patterson finished his cognac and stood to leave.

"That's the end of my sermon," he concluded. "The rest is between you and God. Oh, I almost forgot to give you this," he said and reached into the inside pocket of his jet-black blazer. "I checked your mailbox when I came through the front gate. Thought I'd save you a few steps."

"Thanks for the visit and for delivering the mail, Father," the captain said. "I'll give what you said some thought. And maybe we can do this again sometime."

"I'd like that, Captain," the rector said. "And I look forward to more of that cognac."

"I'll make sure I have some," the captain replied with a grin and extended his hand to the rector to say goodbye at the front door. "And call me Tuck. All my friends do."

"Have a good evening and sleep well, Tuck," the rector said with a sincere smile and shook the retired sailor's hand. "I'll be praying that the Good Lord gives you that wink."

As Father Patterson descended the front steps, Tuck set the mail on the end table beside his chair, returned to his desk, and refilled his glass. Then he took his ivory letter opener from the top drawer and settled back into his chair with the mail in his lap. After another slow sip of cognac, he began shuffling through the mail.

Well, Lord, Tuck thought with a sigh, *if you're really*

listening and you have plans for me, now would be as good a time as any to give me the wink Father Patterson spoke of.

The former captain of the *USS Ronald Reagan* laughed softly at the thought of how simplistic it was to hope for a divine wink in a mundane pile of mail. He felt childish hoping to find a life-changing message among a stack of utility bills and come-ons for vinyl siding and term life insurance. As was his habit, he first sorted the envelopes by size, the largest at the bottom. Then he opened the top-most envelope. Just as he'd guessed, it contained a utility bill. Tuck laughed again, sipped his cognac, and moved on through the stack.

Only when Tuck reached the last and largest envelope did he note its other differences. It was made of fine, white linen paper. He opened it carefully and peered inside at a smaller envelope made of equally fine, royal-blue linen paper. The unique package gave him pause. He took a closer look at the outer envelope. His full name and address were neatly typed on it, along with a simple return address:

Gatcombe Park

Gloucestershire, England

"GATCOMBE PARK?" TUCK ASKED OUT LOUD IN SURPRISE. "What's this about?" he asked as if the sender were in the room with him.

Tuck's best guess was that his old friend, retired British

Royal Navy Captain Martin Edward Michaels, had added him to a list of invitees to what would surely be a grand—but stuffy—royal affair at the rural residence of the captain and his wife, Mary: England's Princess Royal. So he opened it and read it with fond thoughts of his old friends.

AHOY AND A HEARTY HELLO, TUCK!

I hope this letter finds you well and ready for an adventure, because I'm hoping you'll join the Princess and me next month on what is sure to be a fantastically fun ride aboard the world's fastest train. If you think you might still have the grit required for an exhilarating jaunt from Shanghai to London, we'd love to see you again! Please call me when you get this and I'll fill you in.

Your friend in war and peace,

Marty

TUCK READ THE BRIEF LETTER THREE TIMES AND marveled at how short and sweet his friend had kept it after more than a decade of silence between them. He laughed out loud at how very British "an exhilarating jaunt" sounded. And he was surprised that his friend remembered his love of trains. He looked at the clock and was grateful it was too late to call. Before he gave his friend an answer, he needed time to process the thought of a vacation with British royalty. And he certainly needed President Prescott's input at their meeting in the morning.

What Tuck didn't know was that this was far more than a whimsical invitation to a simple train ride. It was, in fact, the prelude to the greatest adventure of his life, a launching pad that would thrust him into the ranks of the "President's Dozen" just as they were called to their deadliest mission ever. No, this was no mere invitation. It was the "wink" Tuck had asked for!

1

W hen Tuck showered and went to bed that evening in Alexandria, Virginia, it was after 4:00 the next morning in Marseille, France, where disgraced ex-French Foreign Legionnaire Alexandre Rafael Bellarose was passed out in a noisy, smoke-filled, foul-smelling after-hours bar aptly named La Ruelle. His head rested in a small puddle of cheap absinthe at the farthest, darkest end of the bar. Everyone was too distracted and making too much noise to hear the thud his skull made when it dropped onto the mahogany bar. And no one noticed the blood trickling from the nasty cut he got on his forehead when his head shattered his glass on the way down.

But the riotous laughter and shouting stopped abruptly when four burly members of the Gendarmerie Nationale military police strode through the door looking for the disgraced and unconscious, court-martialed former member of the French Foreign Legion's 2nd Foreign Parachute Regiment.

"The party's over, Rafe!" a gendarmerie grunted as he helped heft his fallen friend.

"Is he one of yours?" the barman asked as each of the four grabbed a limp arm or leg of the former lieutenant-colonel they still respected and admired.

"Always will be," the nearest legionnaire replied as he helped his comrades lug the massive misfit out the door to the street where a truck waited to transport him to the very commanding officer who just six months earlier had told him he never wanted to see him again.

But collecting Rafe proved to be the easiest part of their mission. It took an hour to transport him to Orange-Caritat Air Base, another hour to get him into the shower, bandage his head wound, and fit his muscular, 6'5" frame into clean civilian clothes suitable to meet with Base Commandant Yves Laurent.

Rafe's head was pounding, but the morning sun warmed his face as he walked across the courtyard to the commandant's office flanked by the gendarmerie who had retrieved him.

"What's this about?" Rafe asked them.

"I have no idea, sir," the sergeant to his left answered while looking straight ahead. "I've never seen anything like this – especially with this commandant. He's normally a brick wall concerning military court decisions. Can't imagine what he wants to talk to you about."

"Well, he's going to have to do all the talking," Rafe grunted. "I've got nothin' to say."

"Considering what it took to find you and bring you here, he must have something important to say to *you*," the sergeant said, still looking straight ahead.

"Good luck, sir," another of the four said quietly as they abruptly left him at the door to the commandant's office.

"Come in!" the commandant barked when Rafe knocked on the door. "Have a seat!" the commandant said a little less aggressively as Rafe stepped inside.

"I think I'll stand," Rafe replied. "I don't plan to be here long. Besides, I thought you never wanted to see me again."

"I didn't," the commandant growled. "Still don't. But this isn't about you and me."

"Well, we're the only two in the room," Rafe noted sarcastically.

"The authority that brought you to my office goes far beyond these walls, Rafe," the commandant told him.

"Don't call me Rafe," the ex-legionnaire shot back. "Only my friends call me that."

"You're right, of course," the commandant conceded. "You proved we weren't friends when you knocked me on my ass last spring. That's why you no longer wear a uniform."

"You earned it!" Rafe said loudly. "Did you call me back for more?"

"I called you back because our country needs you," the commandant said solemnly.

"Bad joke, Commandant!" Rafe snickered and finally sat down.

"This is far from a joke, I assure you," the commandant replied. "In fact, it's serious enough to get your case into a Court of Criminal Appeal and perhaps get you back into uniform."

"After seeing how evil the Legion can be, that's the last thing I want," Rafe said.

"Oh, far worse things could happen, and President DuPris believes the stage might be being set for one of them," the commandant replied as he rose from behind his desk and walked over to a large wall map of the world.

"I couldn't care less," Rafe sneered.

"Just hear me out," the commandant said as he looked at his watch and picked up a laser pointer. "A month from now, the People's Republic of China plans to unveil its next-generation high-speed train by transporting a group of top foreign officials and England's Princess Mary from Shanghai to London in less time than anyone ever dreamed possible until now."

"So?" Rafe replied dismissively.

"The train will travel the length of France from south to north, with a two-hour stop in Paris and a low-speed, thirty-minute chunnel crossing to England," the commandant explained. "We both know high-profile political stunts are prime targets for terrorists."

"So?" Rafe shot back impatiently.

"England has requested that our military not get involved," the commandant said.

"So?" Rafe shot back even more impatiently.

The commandant glanced at his watch again and pushed a button on his laser pointer that transformed the wall map into a flat-screen monitor.

"I'm sure President DuPris can answer that question better than I," the commandant said as Dupris appeared on the screen.

"Salut, Monsieur Bellarose," President DuPris said warmly as Rafe bolted to his feet. "I'm happy to be speaking to you after all I've heard about you. Relax and have a seat, please."

"Speaking with me doesn't often make people happy, Monsieur le Président," Rafe said.

"Don't be so hard on yourself, Legionnaire," DuPris said. "I fear a dark foreign force could be plotting to test France's security, and my advisors tell me you are the patriot best qualified to foil an external threat."

"Didn't you get the memo?" Rafe asked disdainfully. "I've been thrown out of the Legion … and last time I checked, that doesn't happen to patriots."

"As I've already explained to the commandant and officials at the Revisionary Court, that was an unfortunate turn of events for all concerned," DuPris explained. "But as destiny so often does, it seems to have worked in our nation's favor. We need a vigilant, highly-qualified civilian aboard that Chinese bullet train to help ensure it crosses our borders without incident. And as I've already explained, my advisors all agree you're just the man for the job."

"I don't need a job at the moment," Rafe said sarcastically, "which is a good thing because no one will hire a disgraced ex-legionnaire."

"As I've also already explained, I've spoken to the military court about having your court-martial rescinded," DuPris told him. "So I'm hoping that however badly you feel you've been treated by the Legion, you are still the heroic warrior your records say you are and that you still care enough about France to answer her call to duty."

"I'm not sure I care about much of anything anymore,"

Rafe said as he rose from his chair again and headed for the door.

"Do you care that your sister, Madeleine, will be on that train?" DuPris asked.

The question stopped Rafe in his tracks and returned him to his chair.

2

The average horse enthusiast would have called the afternoon a total washout for riding. But U.S. Marshal Quinton "Q" Marshall was unfazed by the fast-approaching rain and rolling thunder when he rode his large, sturdy Appaloosa to the front steps of Madeleine and Noah Allaman's home, just a half-mile from his beloved "Sugar Tree" homestead overlooking picturesque Flathead Lake in Northwestern Montana.

In fact, the weather seemed near-perfect to Q. The wide brim of his Stetson would keep the rain away from the collar of his slicker, and "Montana" and the two cocoa-brown Morgans he had in-tow behind him seemed happy to smell the approaching rain. The aging marshal wasn't too surprised when Noah and Madeleine were no-shows at Sugar Tree for the ride they'd planned the week before. But he *was* surprised that they hadn't called or texted him. So he checked his phone again before dismounting and climbing their broad front steps.

Can't leave, read the text message that had obviously arrived late. *Let yourself in. We're in the basement.*

Q frowned and sighed at the prospect of foregoing a ride in the rain. He hadn't been in the saddle for more than a week, and he and Montana were both overdue for it. But he reluctantly tied the horses to the Allamans' porch railing, climbed the broad front steps, and punched in the six-digit code that unlocked the front door.

"Welcome, cowboy!" Madeleine's voice rang out over the intercom. "You're just in time. C'mon down. The president wants you to hear this too."

Q strode through the kitchen to the basement door and punched in another six-digit code. In the basement, he entered one more code to access the safe room.

"Hey, Q!" Noah and Madeleine said in unison when he entered.

"Hello, Q, my friend!" President Prescott boomed over the ultra-secure video system he'd had installed in the safe rooms of each member of the team he called the President's Dozen.

"I'm way younger than you, Mr. President!" Q replied with a chuckle. "Two years, four months, and six days younger, to be exact! And I'm in a lot better shape than you too!"

"According to the results of my post-reelection physical, I'm fit as a fiddle," the president boomed with a wide grin. "Now, where were we before we were so rudely interrupted?"

"You were explaining the love of trains England's Princess Royal Mary has had since childhood," Madeleine replied.

"Yes, well, believe me, her infatuation with them is still over the top," the president continued. "The story I've been told is that she fell in love with trains on her first ride at six years old when the queen took her along on a trip to Glasgow. She's been a fan and promoter of train travel throughout the six decades since."

"Whoa, how old is the princess?" Noah asked in surprise.

"Seventy years old, this past August," the president said. "Remember, the queen's in her mid-nineties. The queen is also a promoter of the British rail system, and thousands of photos have been published of her and the princess riding on trains."

"That's amazing!" Noah said.

"That's boring!" Q added in his customarily unimpressed way.

"Actually, I have to agree with you for once, Q. It *is* boring," the president conceded. "And no doubt, that's the leverage the Chinese hung their hats on when they invited the princess for a marathon ride aboard their newest high-speed train from Shanghai all the way to London. They claim it can travel at up to 400 miles per hour. But our intelligence pegs it closer to 500. Whichever it is will ensure a 10,000 mile-ride is anything but boring."

"So why are you telling us all this?" Madeleine asked.

"I need to have you and Noah aboard that train when it pulls out of Shanghai," the president said.

"Why?" was all Madeleine could manage to say in her surprise.

"For one, neither of you are American," the president replied. "When Prime Minister Elliott called to tip me to the invitation, he made me promise that I would not try to sneak American civilians or military onboard in Shanghai or at any stops along the route."

"Which explains why Doc and Jenny and Louis aren't here to hear all this," Madeleine concluded out loud.

"Well ... sort of," the president said with obvious hesitation.

"What am I, chopped liver?" Q asked with mock indignation.

"Don't get your briefs in a bunch, Q," the president chuckled. "I only committed to not sneaking Americans aboard at the stations. That leaves some wiggle room between stops."

"I don't imagine 'wiggling's' safe at 400 miles per hour," Noah said.

"We're not at all sure it's even possible," the president said. "But there will be many long stretches of track on which the train will have to reduce speed significantly. And I'm confident Doc and the others—including the old cowboy standing behind you—will come up with a novel strategy to be where we need 'em, when we need 'em, if we need 'em."

"How long is this trip supposed to take?" Q asked.

"A week to ten or eleven days," the president said with a shrug, "depending on a bunch of known and unknown factors."

"That's an awfully long time to spend cooped-up aboard a train," Q said. "The Chinese must be planning activities to break up the monotony."

"I think we can be sure of that," the president agreed. "Not the least of which will be hours of sales pitches to representatives of the UK and other guest countries to buy one or more *Dragons* of their own."

"Which countries, exactly?" Madeleine asked.

"That's a good question," the president admitted. "According to the prime minister, the *Dragon* will likely travel through Nepal, India, Pakistan, Iran, Iraq, Syria, Turkey, Bulgaria, Greece, Germany, Italy, France, and finally England."

"It's surprising the Brits agreed to the trip without an itinerary," Noah said incredulously.

"The princess was so excited about the opportunity, turning down the invitation was not an option," the president said. "Frankly, I can see how Parliament may have found itself in a trick bag on the matter. Britain's rail system sucks, and the princess has made it her life's mission to bring it into the twenty-first century. The prime minister welcomed my offer to help draft a list of foreign invitees to accompany the princess and her husband, retired British Navy Captain Martin Michaels."

"Those two will have their own security and intelligence people aboard, won't they?" Q asked for the record.

"They and some of the other passengers," the president confirmed.

"So what skin do *we* have in this game?" Q asked almost argumentatively.

"China doesn't build anything without military objectives in mind," the president replied. "You can be sure the *Dragon* will be crammed full of the latest, most-highly classified engineering and military hardware and software. That's where you come in, Noah," the president said almost offhandedly.

"Whoa! Wait a minute, Mr. President!" Noah said in a mild panic. "I don't know the first thing about engineering or software!"

"Don't worry about that, Noah," the president replied calmly. "It's the *software* we're after, and I've arranged for you to be shown how to quickly download the data we're interested in."

"You make it sound so easy," Q sighed with a shake of his head. "You know they'll have airtight security onboard."

"But we *don't* know that, Q," the president countered. "We're sure security will be airtight at the stations. But it's unclear what measures will be taken onboard. A lax approach while the *Dragon* is in motion might be a matter of national pride—and a courtesy to the princess and her entourage. And besides, that's where Madeleine comes in."

"What do you mean?" Madeleine asked with relief that she had finally been included.

"My dear, every time you enter the cars of that train, you are going to provide as much, or more, of a distraction as you ever have," the president told her with a devilish grin.

"Now, wait just a minute!" Madeleine said, almost jumping out of her chair. "I resent being used as a bimbo distraction, and I'm offended that you would even think I'd agree to it."

"Frankly, my dear," the president said as gently as he could, "we will only have you and Noah and one other person aboard, and no matter how Noah dresses or wears his hair, he can't hold a candle to the distraction you can provide on your worst day."

"I'll drink to that!" Q blurted out.

"Take it easy," Noah gently told his wife. "The president's right."

"Yeah," Q interjected. "The Chinese will arrest anyone they catch trying to hack their systems, and you don't want Noah to have to live with not being a good distraction, do you?"

"We'll provide the two of you with fake passports and papers to make it appear you don't know one another. Madeleine, it will help if you gradually grow fond of Noah on the trip. But it will also help if you distract the other men onboard. The more you distract them, the better."

"I don't believe this!" Madeleine huffed. "I'll do it, of course," she said. "But I'll start shopping for a new wardrobe tomorrow, and I'll send the bills to the White House, Mr. President."

"It's a deal," the president boomed happily.

"Who's the third person you just referred to?" Q asked.

"Tuck Baird," the president replied. "If he hasn't already, he will soon receive an invitation to make the trip from Princess Mary's husband, Captain Michaels. He and Tuck became good friends during the Falkland Islands War."

"The Falkland Islands War?!" Q repeated. "That's ancient history."

"And that's how far back the two of them go," the president said. "The good Captain Michaels apparently never forgot that Tuck's a sucker for trains, just like the princess. So he called me a few days ago to discuss the idea of inviting Tuck along on the trip. I approved the idea, of course. It's the perfect cover for having an American onboard. I don't believe the Chinese will nix it and risk upsetting the princess. It would sabotage what is obviously a grand propaganda tour to showcase China's engineering dominance."

"Do you really think they'll overlook the fact that Tuck's a member of your administration with military responsibilities?" Q asked cynically.

"They won't have to," the president said quietly. "I asked Tuck for his resignation right after I got off the phone with Captain Michaels. I need to have him on that train, Q. The country needs to have him on that train. We need his experience and intuition on board to assess the possible military applications the *Dragon* presents."

"How'd he take being fired?" Q asked with renewed interest.

"Like a patriot. I did it as gently as I could without tipping him to the invitation," the president explained. "I promised Captain Michaels I wouldn't spoil his surprise. But I'll discuss all this with him when he gets the invitation. I'm confident he'll advise me when he gets it."

"The media will make a big deal out of his tenure being so relatively short," Q noted cynically. "You just know they'll use it to knock you. They will probably say it's a reflection of your leadership style."

"Who cares what the media makes of it?" the president huffed. "They beat that drum all during my first term, and here I sit before you as commander in chief for four more years. If they think I didn't bow to them enough during my first term, they haven't seen anything yet!"

"Attaboy, Mr. President!" Q said cheerfully. "Give 'em hell! They earned it! So what have you got up your sleeve for the rest of the team?" Q asked.

"A whole bunch of thoughts that I'll share with you and Doc and the others over the next couple of days," the president said. "Right now, I've got another meeting to run to. So I'll end this call unless you have a question or two that can't wait."

The trio had no reply.

"Very well! Talk with you tomorrow. I'll have Camilla text you a time to dial in," the president boomed and ended the call.

"Speaking of Doc, have either of you seen or heard from him or Connie today?" Q asked Madeleine and Noah.

"No, now that you mention it," Noah said.

"Me either," Madeleine added.

Q hit *Doc* on his speed dial, and the call went directly to voicemail.

"If this is Q, go away and don't ever call me again … but please leave a message," Doc's voice said with a twinkle.

"Give me a call when ya can," Q barked and hung up. "That's odd," he thought out loud as he slipped his phone into an inside vest pocket. "He can't already be talking with the president, and he never shuts his phone off."

"Maybe he's talking with Louis or Jenny," Madeleine suggested.

"Yeah, maybe," Q mumbled thoughtfully, "but it's not likely. They're vacationing in Georgia with Louis's folks, and you know how Doc hates to interrupt our time off the job."

"Maybe *they* called *him* for some reason," Noah suggested.

"Yeah, you could be right," Q said. "Besides, Doc will call me back soon either way."

"We're done here," Madeleine sighed and ran for the stairs. "Last one upstairs has to make the coffee!"

"I could sure use a cup before headin' back out," Q said. "Wonder if it's still rainin'."

"Was it raining when you got here?" Noah asked as he followed Q upstairs.

"It was just startin'," Q replied.

"They obviously knew what they were doing when they soundproofed the safe rooms they built in our basements," Noah said as he and Q stepped into the kitchen. "It was a dream come true when President Prescott arranged the luxury of being able to send and receive live, encrypted video and audio signals. No more briefing trips to D.C."

"I'll drink to that," Q replied.

"How do you like your coffee?" Noah asked as he put a pot on the stove.

"Irish, please," Q said simply.

"We don't have heavy cream," Noah advised him.

"That's okay," Q chuckled. "It just gets in the way of the whiskey anyway."

Madeleine, Noah, and Q shared small talk and laughs, standing around the big rustic-modern kitchen long enough to finish their coffees. Then Madeleine looked out the large living room window to see if the rain had stopped, and she saw Q's big Appaloosa and two sturdy Morgans tied to the front porch railing.

"Oh my!" she said sorrowfully. "When the president called, I completely forgot that we were supposed to join you for a ride. The rain's stopped, and I'm still up for it if you are, Q."

"Me too!" Noah added enthusiastically.

"Sure!" Q answered. "I'm going to ride Montana over to Doc and Connie's place while you two get ready. Come on over when you're saddled up."

"Sounds like a plan!" Noah said as he rinsed the coffee cups and loaded them into the dishwasher. "We'll be right behind you."

As Q climbed onto Montana, he pondered possible reasons Doc might have for not returning his call, and he felt uneasy with the thoughts that entered his mind. But he pushed them aside and hoped for the best as he sent Montana into a full gallop toward his closest friends' lake house. As the house came into view, the rain began to fall again, and a loud clap of thunder gave him and Montana both a jolt of adrenalin.

Even at 100 yards away, Q could see the house was dark, and the front door was slightly ajar. Fifty yards out, he slowed Montana to a walk and sized up the silent scene as best he could with what he could see. The light from a huge, angry thunderbolt shown through the windows of the lake house, but Q didn't catch sight of anyone's silhouette inside. He didn't like what his gut told him, and he undid the strap that secured his .357 Magnum Colt Python revolver in its holster and flipped its safety off. As he dismounted, he pulled his U.S.

Marshal badge from his side vest pocket and hung it around his neck. He ascended the stairs to the porch without a sound and nudged the front door with a boot just hard enough to quietly swing it wide open.

"U.S. Marshal!" he announced.

Q heard only a deafening silence. He entered the dark living room slowly to give his eyes a chance to adjust. When he was just two steps in, another bolt of lightning illuminated the room, and he caught sight of someone sitting on the sofa out of the corner of his eye. He wheeled toward the figure with his Python raised and cocked.

"Turn on the lamp beside you!" Q ordered, and the figure slowly complied.

In the light, Q got his first look at a slender 19- or 20-year-old man he didn't recognize seated at the far end of the sofa with a 22 caliber Smith & Wesson pistol in his lap. Q figured the young man must either be high or mentally handicapped when he slowly raised the pistol and pointed it in the marshal's direction.

"You know, young fella, there are days when I almost hope for an opportunity to shoot someone. Lucky for you, today ain't one of 'em. So slowly put that gun on the floor, stand up, and raise your hands."

The young man complied and stared blankly at Q, waiting to be told what to do next.

"Let's take a little tour of the house," Q said as he

reached out and pushed the silent stranger in the direction of the kitchen.

It was empty and ransacked. So were the pantry, the study, two small bedrooms, and the half-bath between the study and Connie's craft room. That left just the laundry room and the master bedroom on the first floor. The laundry room was as clean and neat as Connie always kept it, but when his captive balked at opening the door of the master bedroom, Q began to fear what he might be about to discover.

"Open it!" the marshal commanded as he pulled back the Python's hammer and braced himself for whatever came next.

The young intruder slowly pushed the door open to reveal Doc and Connie bound and unconscious in two wingback chairs. Q recalled that his wife, Marsha, had found the chairs in an antique shop while the lake house was being built. She reupholstered them as a housewarming present. He was thankful she did not see how they were used at that moment.

"Doc! Wake up, Doc!" Q shouted as he shook his friend by the shoulders. "Connie! Doc! Wake up!"

"They'll be out a while," a voice said from behind Q as he felt a gun barrel pressed against the back of his skull. "Drop the gun and don't turn around," the voice said firmly. "Do what you're told, and everyone just might get out of this alive."

"What the hell is this about?" Q asked as calmly as he

could and hoped the mention of survival ruled out a crime of revenge. "Do you want money? I paid over $3,000 for that Colt. Any pawn shop in the area will give you at least a grand."

"Money ain't all we're lookin' for," the cocky voice told him. "A house like this must have a lot more in it than just money. How do you know these two?"

"They're friends," Q grunted. "And I can tell you there's no future in treating my friends like this."

"Keep talking like that, and you might be the one with no future!" the voice spat back.

"You said nobody'd get hurt," blurted the young man Q had found in the living room.

"No one has ... yet!" the cocky voice shouted back at him.

"Well, Marshal," a third voice said, "if you're such good friends with these two, you must know what's in the basement. That's our next stop. So move it!"

Q quickly walked through the kitchen toward the basement door. He knew that Noah and Madeleine would arrive sometime soon, and he didn't want the intruders to see them. So he quickly entered the six-digit code and opened the door. On the way through the door, Q flipped the switch beside the knob that would automatically close and lock the door in ten minutes. The soundproof safe room also had a lock with a six-digit code that Q also knew by heart. Neither

Q nor anyone else in the President's Dozen understood how he could recall the unique codes, but he could somehow. And he was grateful for it that day. He breathed a sigh of relief when he led the intruders into the safe room and closed the door before Noah and Madeleine arrived.

"So what do they keep in here?" the cockiest of the criminals barked at Q.

"I don't know, exactly," Q lied. "But I always figured they must have built this fancy room to hide somethin' worth an awful lot. There's probably a safe or two in the floor, under the desk, or behind the pictures or monitors on the walls."

As Q stalled, he watched for a tiny LED to flash along the edge of the desk. It finally flashed when Noah and Madeleine entered the front door of the house while the intruders were ripping up carpet and pulling the pictures and monitors off the walls.

"Doc?! Q?!" Noah shouted into the stone-still silence.

"Connie, are you here?!" Madeleine shouted with an urgency bordering on panic.

"They must all be in the basement," Noah thought out loud when he looked into the kitchen from the living room, then headed toward it with Madeleine at his elbow.

"What do you guys think you're going to find down here?" the two of them heard Q ask over the intercom.

"If you were *real* thieves, you'd already know what you were looking for and where to find it. Only amateurs would waste precious time tearing the place apart, hoping to find something worth stealing."

Noah and Madeleine knew Q must be in the safe room with dangerous company and that he had turned the intercom on to warn them. But neither of them had brought their pistols along, and there was obviously no time to return home for them. Noah suddenly remembered the longsword he and Madeleine had given Doc on his last birthday and that Doc mounted it above the fireplace in his study. Noah quickly retrieved it, but in his haste, he neglected to check the other rooms and missed seeing Doc and Connie unconscious in their bedroom. When he rejoined Madeleine in the kitchen, his sole focus was to save Q.

Madeleine gasped when the basement door closed and locked behind them as they descended the stairs. She knew it could not be reopened without the required code, which only Q knew. But she also knew she and Noah weren't leaving the basement without him anyway.

"They still don't know we're here," Madeleine whispered to her husband when they reached the basement.

"But they soon will!" Noah whispered back as he and Madeleine took positions on either side of the safe room door and waited for the intruders to exit with Q in tow.

"There ain't no damn safe in here!" they heard an intruder shout. "You said there was!"

"I said there might be," they heard Q correct him. "You fellas ain't too smart, are ya?"

"We're wastin' time down here, Joe!" Noah and Madeleine heard another intruder shout. "Let's take this guy's Colt and get outta here!"

"Well, at least one of you has an ounce of sense!" they heard Q wisecrack.

"Yeah, Joe! Let's get outta here!" they heard a young vice say next.

"That makes two of you with some sense," Q sarcastically added. "Why not make it unanimous and stop pointing those guns at me and get outta here?"

"Okay, let's go!" the one who must have been Joe shouted, and Noah and Madeleine braced for the mayhem that was about to erupt.

When they heard the beeps of Q entering the code to unlock the door, Madeleine crouched low, and Noah held the longsword chest-high in both hands like a Major League slugger holds a bat. Q came out first with a small smile on his face as he caught sight of his two teammates lying in wait. He crouched low like Madeleine and wheeled around to help however he could. With Q out of the way, Noah swung the longsword into the chest of the one he guessed was Joe. The sword's razor edge cut into the thief's upper arms and chest and sent him reeling back into his unsuspecting partners.

For the next few seconds, Noah, Madeleine, and Q ducked, bobbed, and weaved to avoid being hit by the wildly ricocheting bullets the bandits fired at no particular targets. As the one called Joe reached for what Noah guessed was a second gun inside his shirt, the expert swordsman lunged just like he had trained for the past seven years and thrust the longsword a half-inch into the center of the thief's chest.

"Aaaaaahhhhhh!" Joe cried out as the scalpel-like point pierced his sternum.

"Aw, shut up!" Q shouted. "You act like you just got stabbed with a sword for cryin' out loud! Anyone else want some of this?!" he shouted at the other two, who quickly gave up.

"Are you okay, Q?" Madeleine asked while she and Noah picked up the weapons and bound the trio's wrists and ankles with zip ties Noah always carried in a pocket of his pants.

"I'm a whole lot better than these three," he shot back with a laugh. "Damn! I almost forgot about Doc and Connie!" he gasped and raced upstairs.

"Where are they?" Madeleine called out as she and Noah bolted up the stairs behind Q.

"Follow me!" he shouted back as he ran toward the master bedroom.

Q was untying Connie when Madeleine and Noah caught up with him, and they worked to free Doc. He and Connie began waking up while being freed.

"Oh, thank God you found us!" Connie cried out as Madeleine called 9-1-1.

"Be careful!" Doc then shouted. "They may still be in the house!"

"Oh, they're still in the house all right!" Q chuckled. "But thanks to Madeleine and Noah, everything's under control. As you often do, you missed the best part of the operation, Doc," Q good-naturedly taunted his best friend.

"Where's Timmy?" Doc asked anxiously. "Is Timmy okay?"

"Who's Timmy?" Q asked with some confusion.

"He's a young guy who does our landscaping," Doc told him. "Connie and I were talking with him in the kitchen when these guys broke in, and … and … that's the last I can remember."

"How old is Timmy?" Q asked with the youngest of the three intruders in mind.

"He's twenty, but developmentally he's about twelve," Doc told him.

"Is he about 5'10" with short blond hair?" Q asked cautiously.

"That's him!" Doc said excitedly. "Is he okay? Is he here?"

"Yeah, he's okay, and he's still here," Q replied cryptically. "But he's tied up at the moment. You'll see him in a little bit."

"Oh, thank God!" Connie sighed as Q freed her. "He's easily confused, and I don't know what we'd do if he'd been hurt by the thugs who broke in on us."

"Yeeeah, well, there's a little more you two need to know about all that," Q hesitantly replied and rubbed the back of his neck.

"What's that supposed to mean?" Doc asked with concern.

"I'm not sure myself," Q replied honestly. "But we'll let the sheriff's department untangle it all and fill us in later. In the meantime, Madeleine and Noah and I will just focus on getting you and Connie untangled. Okay?"

"You're the boss," Doc sighed.

"Well, *that's* a first!" Q said as another thunderbolt shook the house, and the rain returned.

3

THE POTENTIAL SIDEWAYS DOWNSIDE

As a hulking, black Suburban entered the north gate to the White House grounds with Tuck aboard, he reread the invitation he'd received from his friend, Captain Michaels. The prospect of a ride across two continents on the fastest high-speed train in the world excited him. But he had begun to wonder if he'd truly been invited to enjoy a luxury rail vacation, courtesy of an old friend with the best of intentions, or if he was being drawn into a dangerous international covert operation—seduced with a ripe, juicy carrot into an intelligence operation that could cost him and others their lives.

He was elated for the first few hours after the invitation arrived. But the more he thought about it, the more he began to suspect it was somehow linked to the president's request for his resignation. His knowledge that there are few coincidences in Washington, D.C., overpowered his hopes that there was a simple explanation. Even if the good captain had innocently included him among the invitees as an opportunity for them to reconnect, Tuck knew the Brits must have consulted the president before they mailed the invitation. He also knew the president was better at keeping secrets than anyone else he'd ever served with.

If indeed there was a mission afoot, Tuck knew the president would have to launch it soon. So he decided to force the issue and mention the invitation at the outset of their meeting.

"Good morning, Tuck!" the president boomed in his familiar way. "How are you today?"

"I'm great, Mr. President. How about you?" Tuck asked to get the president talking.

"I'm happy to get the morning started by meeting with you, Tuck," the president said. "I wasn't exactly forthcoming when I asked you to step down. But I knew we were set to meet first thing this morning to discuss the particulars, and I wanted to get a few loose ends in order first."

"Loose ends?" Tuck asked with a raised eyebrow. "I hope I wasn't the cause."

"Oh, no!" the president assured him. "On the contrary. Your performance has been stellar. In fact, that's the reason I'm so comfortable with this transition I have in mind for you. And I needed to speak with a few of your counterparts before I discussed it with you."

"Transition?" Tuck asked as his eyebrow raised even higher. "I'm not sure I'm cut out for any other role here, Mr. President. To be completely honest with you, the idea of returning to retirement grew quite appealing overnight."

"Yeah, I have nights like that, too," the president said, looking past Tuck out onto the south lawn outside the Oval Office. "If you don't mind, take a walk with me out on the lawn. It frees my mind to walk in the fresh air—and it's the one place I can really speak my mind at this address, if you know what I mean."

"Let's do it," Tuck said as he sprang to his feet, wondering what it was the president was going to "speak freely" about while they avoided being recorded.

"Please, hold my calls for a bit, Camilla," the president simply said into his intercom before leading Tuck out onto the lawn. "It's beautiful out here, isn't it?" the president asked and filled his lungs with the warm morning air. On days like today, I'd like to move the Resolute onto the grass with no phone line and just work on everything out here—including my tan."

"So you *are* human, Mr. President," Tuck chuckled. "Alert the media!"

"They'll never believe it!" the president boomed with his familiar broad smile and led Tuck to the fountain at the far end of the south lawn.

"It's easy to forget the grounds are this big," Tuck noted

as they neared the fountain, and he looked back at the White House.

"I'm glad they are," the president said. "It's remote but secure ... which, by the way, is why I asked to meet with you this morning."

"Why is that, Mr. President?" Tuck asked in a calm voice that belied his anxiety with how long it was taking the president to get to the point.

The president sat on the edge of the fountain basin with his arms crossed and said, "I've heard you're among a select group of people from various countries who have been invited to join Britain's Princess Royal Mary and her husband aboard the fastest train in the world. You are apparently even better connected than our records indicate."

"I don't know if I'd describe it as 'connected' exactly, Mr. President," Tuck said. "British Navy Captain Marty Michaels and I crossed paths and hit it off during the Falklands War, and we've stayed in touch over the years. It began long before he ever met and married the princess. Captain Michaels is someone I would call well-connected."

"I'd say that anybody who calls him 'Marty' is well-connected too," the president insisted. "So, are you going?" the president finally asked.

"I have to tell you, I tried very hard to be coolheaded about whether or not to accept the invitation," Tuck confided to the president. "Oh sure, I've been nuts about trains ever since the first one showed up under the Christmas tree when I was eight years old. But I'm a bit older now, and I have more important things to do than taking a train ride. That is, *I did have* … until you fired me, Mr. President."

"I didn't fire you, Tuck," the president said. "I need you in a different capacity that's more hands-on, more urgent—and in the interest of full disclosure—potentially more dangerous."

Tuck let the president's words sink in for a long moment, then sat beside him atop the low fountain wall and assumed the same position: legs straight, ankles and arms crossed.

"If I understand you correctly, you're suggesting that my choice is to either retire and spend the rest of my days in a comfortable rocking chair on my front porch in Alexandria or go on this train ride and potentially spend my remaining days in a squalid Chinese prison. Is that correct, Mr. President?" Tuck asked, looking directly into the president's eyes.

"Well, since we're down to brass tacks, that's not quite the worst-case scenario," the president admitted. "I'm sure you know that if things go sideways, the Chinese could send you to a worse—and far more final—fate."

"Now that we've discussed the brass tacks, give me the nuts and bolts," Tuck said frankly.

"The Chinese call the train the *Dragon*. It's an engineering and cyber marvel," the president began.

"Our intelligence on the ground in and around China's proving grounds tell us the *Dragon* is capable of reaching more than 500 miles per hour under ideal conditions. It's larger yet lighter and stronger than anything engineered in the West. Its magnetic levitation system suspends it above the track. And it barely needs to slow down while its mag-lev suspension combines seamlessly with a groundbreaking wheel system that adjusts to ride on all rail gauges. The train's compartments are pressurized and nearly soundproof for the quietest, most comfortable ride ever achieved by trains."

"Sounds to me like a simple case of the East beating the West in yet another vital sector of the economy," Tuck said with a shrug. "We'll catch up quickly. We always do. In the meantime, what possible difference can I make by taking one ride on the *Dragon*? And what do you have in mind that could upset the Chinese enough to lock me up or shoot me?"

"The *Dragon* is a huge leap in transporting equipment and personnel," the President explained. "And China is refining it at a furious clip. If, as our Joint Chiefs believe, China has long-term plans to dominate neighboring countries. Imagine what they could achieve with the support of a network of trains moving military hardware and troops from one region to another—one country to another and one continent to another—at nearly the speed of sound without leaving the ground and without the need for diesel fuel."

"It would be an infantry commander's dream come true, for sure," Tuck agreed. "But dreams and reality are very different things, and it's hard to believe that Chinese engineers have wed the two so incredibly. Like, for instance, how does it run where there are no electric lines?"

"I have no idea, Tuck," the president assured him. "But they're so confident in the train that they plan to showcase it to the entire world. And believe me, the world will watch closely. You can bet Beijing's plans for the trip far exceed its stated purpose. Every government this trip convinces to convert to a *Dragon*-class rail system will spend billions upgrading their rail system infrastructures and roll out a bright red carpet to welcome the *Dragon*."

"But China's leaning more toward capitalism every day, just as the West has encouraged them to do for the past three decades," Tuck noted. "So what's the problem?"

"Honestly, Tuck, we're not sure," the president admitted. "That's where you come in. You'll be the only American aboard. I'm counting on your military background to help us assess just how militaristic this promotional push is. So I'm asking you to accept the invitation and go along with the princess and your friend Captain Michaels, then simply keep your eyes and ears open to the comings and goings of military personnel on board. It will be helpful to know if they're just providing security or if they're being consulted in conversations between Chinese representatives and members of the foreign delegations on the trip."

"That's it?" Tuck asked in surprise. "You just want me to observe and report? It sounds like something someone else can do—and get locked up for—every bit as well as me. So the rocking chair on my porch still looks pretty good at the moment, Mr. President."

"That brings me to the other half of the mission," the president said.

"Which is?" Tuck asked.

"Doc and his team will help ensure the trip doesn't go sideways," the president answered.

"You mean they'll help ensure I don't get locked away in a Chinese jail," Tuck added.

"Or worse…" The president sighed.

"Count me in!" Tuck said emphatically.

"I admire decisive people," the president said and extended his hand for a shake.

"And you know how much I admire Doc and his team," Tuck said as they shook hands. "I'm not about to pass up a mission with them."

"I should have mentioned it at the start," the president said with a twinkle in his eye. "It would have saved us a lot of time."

"True, but I *do* appreciate knowing the potential

sideways downside," Tuck said with a grin and a twinkle of his own.

Half an hour later, Tuck put his signed letter of resignation on the president's desk and headed for the West Wing portico, where the gleaming black Suburban awaited him. He walked down the corridor slowly to take in his last few rarefied moments as a White House insider and punched Captain Michaels's number into his cell phone.

"Hello, Marty!" he said cheerfully when his old friend came on the line. "Yeah, it's Tuck calling to gratefully and enthusiastically accept your invitation to spend what I'm certain will be an absolutely wonderful time with you and the princess!"

Their conversation lasted half the ride back to Alexandria, and Tuck was elated by the time he ended the call. He knew the trip would be one of the most memorable of his life. And predictably, he wished Eleanor were going with him. He smiled when he recalled how she often told him he needed to get away more—how they both did—and he knew she'd think a 10,000-mile journey aboard the fastest train ever built with England's princess royal couple would be the adventure of a lifetime. Despite that happy thought, or maybe because of it, he was sad that she would not be along on the trip. But at the same time, he was excited about getting out from behind a desk and being sent on a covert mission halfway around the world with the President's Dozen.

Tuck stepped from the Suburban onto his driveway in a jumble of melancholy and exhilaration. As he crossed his manicured front lawn, he recalled how Father Patterson had encouraged him with the assurance that life-changing events can happen when they're least expected ... and most needed. The thought moved him to call the rector right there in the middle of his front yard, awash in the bright afternoon sunlight.

"Hello, Father Patterson!" Tuck happily began his voicemail message. "I just wanted to let you know that I got the wink you told me would happen if I asked for it. I don't want to go overboard and say it's made me a believer. So I'll just say that I'm no longer a doubter. If I could afford it, I'd send you a bottle of Remy Martin Louis XIII. But since I just lost my job, that's not gonna happen. Call me back when you can, and we'll figure out when we can get together at my place again and empty the bottle we started. Thanks again, Father! And, oh, ugh, God bless!"

THINGS WEREN'T GOING AS SMOOTHLY FOR RAFE Bellarose, who was literally rooming in a

janitor's closet at Orange-Caritat Air Base near the city of Saguenay in south-central France. But even that was a step up from his recent rock bottom. He was sober, had access to hot showers, a couple of changes of clean clothes, and three hot meals a day, courtesy of French president DuPris, who'd recently realized his nation still needed Rafe's extraordinary skills as an ex-foreign legionnaire. Fortunately for France, the decorated war hero's abilities and love of country were still intact despite months of binge-drinking in a futile effort to numb the pain of his court-martial and ejection from the legion for assaulting a fellow officer.

It wasn't that simple, of course. Rafe wasn't initially inclined to accept President DuPris' request for his help providing security aboard the *Dragon*. He wasn't the least bit moved by the challenge of safeguarding a trainload of government officials from other nations, including England's Princess Royal Mary and her husband, while they were on French soil. But DuPris had played his wild card: Rafe's younger sister, Madeleine Allaman, a member of U.S. President Prescott's most elite special operations team, would be aboard the train.

So Rafe agreed to ride the *Dragon*. The wonder train would not take on passengers once it left Beijing, which meant he would have to board in China and stand watch the entire 16,000-kilometer trip. French officials prepared a fake passport and supporting documents identifying him as Jacques Saint-Pallet, a travel writer for *La Figaro*, France's largest newspaper.

For the first time on any mission, he'd carry no weapons. China had made it clear there would be highly trained security personnel and state-of-the-art technology on board the *Dragon*. They insisted the *Dragon* be recognized as sovereign Chinese territory, the equivalent of a mobile embassy. Each host nation would, of course, take security measures in and around the stations the *Dragon* would pass through. But once the *Dragon* left each station, China's Ministry of State Security would provide the only security for the *Dragon* and its passengers.

So Rafe figured that for most of the trip, especially outside of France, he need only look out for his sister. Other than that, he would stay alert to visual and verbal clues that suggested potential terrorist threats to the *Dragon* and its passengers. It was relatively routine duty, really. Though uncomfortable with his lack of weapons, Rafe was confident he'd overcome any challenges using whatever weapons he could find or devise. It was, after all, the tactic he was most known for as a legionnaire.

There was a catch, however. He hadn't spoken with his sister since before his court-martial. Prior to that, their communication had been spotty to nonexistent while they both were involved in covert activities on opposite sides of the Atlantic. With the exception of a short time they'd spent working together on a joint mission nearly three years earlier, neither of them knew much about what the other had been up to lately. Rafe knew he had to quickly change that if he was serious about keeping her safe aboard the *Dragon*. So he headed for the mess hall, where he knew he'd find a secure office phone to call her.

"Hello? Who's calling, please?" Madeleine asked because her caller ID was blank.

"Hi, Sis! It's Rafael!" Rafe told his kid sister. "How have you been? I know it's been a while since we last spoke, and I just wanted to check in on you and hear your voice. I miss you."

"Oh, my god, I miss you, too, Rafael!" Madeleine told him excitedly. "Is everything alright? I've tried calling you many times, and your phone went directly to your voicemail, which is always full, of course."

"You've probably heard that I hit a patch of bad luck a little while ago," Rafe said. "But I'm doing much better now. I understand you're taking quite a train ride, and I wanted to let you know that I'll be on board as well."

"You will!?!" Madeleine asked even more excitedly. "Oh, my gosh, that's fantastic news! But I am not supposed to know anyone on board. So we'll have to pretend to be strangers. How fun it will be pretending to meet you for the very first time!"

"That should be easy enough since I've practically been a stranger for some time now," Rafe admitted.

"Never mind all that," Madeleine said. "Let's just focus on this chance we have to reconnect. You know, there just might be a very helpful freedom in speaking to one another as strangers on a train."

"Who else will be there with you?" Rafe asked.

"Noah, but he will be a stranger too," Madeleine replied.

"No others?" Rafe asked with surprise.

"Not sure at the moment," Madeleine said. "And as much as President Prescott speaks with DuPris, you may know before I do. So let's stay in touch. Why didn't you use your phone to call me?"

"I threw it in the Seine a while ago," Rafe told her.

"You definitely have anger issues, big brother," Madeleine shook her head and told him.

"I've never claimed otherwise," Rafe replied. "And lately, I guess I have more than ever. I've got to go now, Sis. Say hi to Noah—and Doc, when you see him. Love you! Au revoir!"

"Au revoir, big brother. Love you too!" Madeleine replied, and Rafe ended the call.

As Rafe hung up the phone, one of the gendarmeries who had rounded him up the night before stuck his head into the office.

"Hey, Rafe!" he shouted like an old friend. "The commandant wants to speak with you in his office right away."

Rafe ambled out of the office and through the kitchen, snatched an apple, a knife, and a slice of Reblochon cheese, and headed outside to the truck that was waiting to transport him across the base to the commandant's office.

"What's this about?" Rafe asked the driver.

"Don't know," the driver replied. "Nobody knows much

about you or why you're here. Why *are* you here? Can you talk about it?"

"No," Rafe said flatly.

"Not at all?" the driver asked again.

Rafe bit into his apple and shot the driver a look that made it clear he didn't want to talk.

"Hello again, Rafael. Did you sleep well?" the commandant asked in an effort to move past the hostile history they shared.

"I'll bet you didn't send for me to ask that," Rafe said sarcastically.

"No, actually, your new passport and papers have arrived," the commandant said and handed Rafe a large envelope. "Passengers will likely ask you about your experiences as a travel writer. I think it would be wise to tell them you primarily travel throughout North and Central America. That should help you avoid questions about why you're not more familiar with the accommodations and attractions in various European cities."

"Sounds reasonable," Rafe said simply. "Anything else?"

"In about an hour, you will be transported to INTERPOL headquarters in Lyon for a briefing," the commandant explained.

"I'll be ready and waiting at the front gate," Rafe said abruptly. "Is that all?"

"Look, Rafael," the commandant said and rocked back in his chair, "I just want you to know that I've gotten past what happened between us, and I bear you no hard feelings."

"Anything else?" Rafe coldly asked again.

"Godspeed, Rafael," the commandant said sincerely.

Rafe abruptly exited the office, and the commandant rubbed his forehead in exasperation. He regretted having been involved in the events that resulted in Rafe's court-martial. But Rafe's actions were inexcusable, and the court-martial was unavoidable. The commandant felt that the legion and the nation lost at least as much as Rafe did when the verdict was handed down. He was remorseful about the negative impact it had on Rafe's life and legacy as a patriot and a hero.

Standing at his office window, he watched Rafe interact with legionnaires as he walked across the base. It was obvious the once-celebrated hero still had the heart of a legionnaire. The commandant was comforted by the certainty that no court or conviction could ever tarnish the shining spirit of the warrior who had stood before him just moments before ... and would hopefully do so again when this mission was completed.

4

A FEARSOME LOGISTICAL ADVANTAGE

U.S. Marine Sergeant Major Louis Danforth and his wife, Chief Warrant Officer 5 Jennifer Perry-Danforth, were stepping out of a Secret Service Suburban in their dress blues beneath the East Wing of the White House, anxious to hear why President Prescott had summoned them from their vacation on the Georgia coast.

"I thought Doc and the others would greet us," Louis whispered to his wife as they walked down the hallway toward the stairway that led to Camilla's office, just outside the Oval.

"Ahhh, the two best-dressed members of my Dozen!" the president boomed as he stood beside Camilla's desk with Tuck. "Welcome back! I'm sorry to have interrupted your well-deserved vacation. But as you must have guessed, something's come up."

"No problem, sir," Louis answered. "It's good to be back, actually! Hi, Camilla! Hi, Tuck! It's been a while!"

"Yes, it has, Louis," Tuck said as he matched salutes with the Sergeant Major and his Chief Warrant Officer 5 bride.

"Welcome home," Camilla chimed in, "or at least, your home away from home."

"We're raring to go, Mr. President!" Jenny said in her excitement to be back in action.

"You haven't even heard what the mission is yet," the president chuckled.

"Whatever it is, it's what we signed up for," Louis quickly replied.

"Roger that!" his wife added.

"Follow me, then," the president said and led the trio to the Situation Room elevator.

"Are Doc and the others already here?" Jenny asked on the four-story ride down.

"In a way," the president said.

"*In a way?* You mean they're online?" Louis asked.

"I wouldn't call it that, exactly," the president answered cryptically. "We finally worked all the kinks out of the cyber network we created exclusively for your team, and I think you'll be impressed with the result."

"Welcome back!" Situation Room Director Chance Oliver happily shouted to Jenny and Louis when the president led them out of the elevator. "How was Georgia?"

"It's still very Southern!" Jenny said with a smile. "I'm ready for Midwest cuisine."

"I know a place that has the best Coney Island-style hotdogs this side of Detroit," Oliver said with a grin. "I'll buy whenever the president turns you loose."

"It's a deal!" Louis quickly said.

"They better have buckets of chopped onions," Jenny added with a smile.

"No romance for me tonight!" Louis chuckled.

"But right now, it's time to impress you both," the president boomed as he stepped over to a ten-foot turntable at the center of the floor. "Has everyone checked in?" he asked Oliver.

"They have, Mr. President!" Oliver replied excitedly and flipped the *On Air* switch on his huge control console.

"Hello, everyone!" the president boomed even louder than usual. "Are you ready for our first virtual experience?"

"Hello, Mr. President!" Doc's voice resonated over the room's surround sound system. "As always, we're ready, willing, and able!"

"Okay, Oliver," the president told the director with a wink and a nod. "Beam them in!"

"*Abracadabra!*" Oliver said with a flare as he flipped a second switch labeled *Present.*

Instantly, life-size, 3-D, holographic images of Doc, Q, Noah, and Madeleine appeared standing at the center of the turntable. Q was reclined in an anti-gravity chair beside them, puffing on a Cohiba Robustos cigar, wearing a Hawiian shirt, broad-striped Bermuda shorts, Oakley Radar EV Path sunglasses, a Diamante Stetson, and Dollar Store flip-flops.

"Welcome, team!" the president boomed with arms spread wide. "Can you all see me?

"Plain as day!" Doc said, and the others agreed. "Hello, everybody!"

"Perfect!" the president boomed with obvious joy. "I hope I didn't interrupt anything important, Q. Are you comfortable enough for this meeting?"

"Like a bug in a rug, Mr. President," Q replied. "I've got steaks on the barbie, but I dialed the flame down. So we're good for at least twenty or thirty minutes."

"Well, I'll try to hurry through this as best I can," the president said with a grin. "Give 'em a slow spin, Corporal," he told Oliver, who set the turntable into a gentle rotation, which gave those in the Situation Room the effect of walking around Doc and his team.

"This is just too amazing!" Jenny gushed.

"It's the latest wonder of the cyber age!" the president said proudly. "Every home should have one! But let's move into a soundproof room and get down to business."

The president led Louis and Jenny into the room. Doc and the others were already in their Montana safe rooms.

"The hologram is a showstopper, for sure," the president said. "But this is still the place where we get the show on the road, if you know what I mean."

"*We do*, Mr. President," Doc answered. "I'm sure that hologram projection will have interesting applications. But I feel more able to speak freely now."

"Roger that!" Louis agreed.

"Personally, I never have a problem speaking freely," Q wisecracked.

"It would be nice if you did every now and then," Doc said wistfully.

"So, why have you called us together, Mr. President?" Louis asked as he and Jenny settled into chairs across a metal table from their commander in chief.

"I need you to help protect a dragon," the president said solemnly. "Or I should say, *the Dragon*—the fastest train on the planet. I've already told Q, Madeleine, and Noah a bit about it."

"Where is it?" Doc asked.

"At the moment, it's in Shanghai, being prepped for a high-profile marathon promotional tour," the president answered.

"What do we care whether a Chinese train is secure or not?" Doc asked.

"I personally couldn't give a ..." Q started to say.

"Knock it off, Q!" Doc cut Q off firmly. "Let's hear the president out."

"I know how you feel, Q," the president said. "And lots of our fellow Americans feel the same way. But the *Dragon*—and the trip it's about to take—pose a potential threat to our national security."

"Then why aren't we trying to stop it?" Jenny asked.

"Because we can't," the president replied matter-of-factly. "The Chinese are promoting the *Dragon* as the most advanced, commercial, high-speed mag-lev train in the world," he explained as he clicked a tiny remote, and the lights dimmed while the walls of the room lit up with a bootlegged copy of China's promotional video of a *Dragon* prototype racing through the Chinese countryside. "You and the others online can't appreciate this video, Doc," the president explained. "But believe me, it's impressive."

"Holy shit!" Tuck forgot himself and exclaimed when he saw it. "That's the *Dragon?*"

"That's it!" the president said with obvious envy. "You're watching nearly one mile of the sleekest, most advanced technology and engineering. It's traveling at an average speed approaching 400 miles per hour on a test track in the Chinese countryside south of Shanghai, in the Zhejiang province."

"I can see why the Chinese named it the *Dragon*. It actually looks like something alive and mythical as it winds through the landscape," Jenny marveled. "It's so streamlined. And its long, raking nose slopes dramatically to track level, as though it's visually following the track. It's absolutely beautiful in the bright sunlight!"

"Is there no audio?" Tuck asked the president.

"Oh, yes," the president said as he admired the image before them. "You're hearing it. I'll turn the volume up, and if you listen closely, you can hear the wind rushing past the camera, which was mounted on a chopper that hovered about two hundred feet above the track. The *Dragon* can't be heard at that distance."

"That's absolutely incredible!" Louis said as he stared at the scene.

"How fast is it actually moving?" Doc asked.

"Our experts pegged this run at an average of 420 miles per hour," the president said.

"How in the hell can something that big move that fast?" Noah asked softly.

"It uses electromagnetic levitation technology," the president explained. "There's no friction to slow it down because it never actually touches the track it runs on. Instead, it hovers roughly a half-inch above the track at all times."

"Are you sure this video was shot at real speed and not altered?" Q asked skeptically.

"We're positive," the president assured him. "And that's the problem."

"What do you mean?" Doc asked.

"This video confirms the Chinese have not exaggerated their claims of having created the world's fastest train. We believe it can exceed 500 miles per hour."

"What's it weigh?" Tuck asked.

"That will depend on how many cars are ultimately coupled," the president said. "The one you're looking at has fifteen cars. If it were carrying the maximum amount of passengers and luggage and another five cars for the crew and security personnel, it would weigh approximately 7,500 tons. The *Dragon* being prepped for the tour will be about a mile long."

"A one-mile-long train moving at more than 400 miles per hour? That's not possible!" Q blurted out.

"It's not possible anywhere but in China," the president corrected him. "And China's about to set the *Dragon* free, which brings me to the point of this meeting."

"He takes almost as long to get to the point as you do, Doc!" Q wisecracked.

"Please continue, Mr. President," Doc said sharply.

"The *Dragon* is about to leave China," President Prescott announced.

"Where's it going?" Jenny asked.

"London, England," the president said matter-of-factly.

"For a minute there, I thought you said London, England," Doc chuckled in disbelief.

"Don't check your hearing aids, Doc," the president laughed. "You heard me just fine."

"But…but London's halfway around the world from China," Doc stuttered.

"Just a little over 16,000 kilometers … more than 10,000 U.S. miles … depending on the route they've selected." Madeleine finally joined the conversation.

"We don't know the route yet?" Doc asked in obvious surprise.

"We have a good idea," the president clarified. "But security is very tight because there will be high-profile passengers aboard, and the entire world will be following this momentous excursion, which makes the *Dragon* a prime target for terrorist groups."

"And who are the high-profile passengers?" Doc asked with squinted eyes.

"England's Princess Royal Mary and her husband, retired British Navy Captain Martin Michaels," the president answered. "But most important to us, the royal couple has invited Tuck to accompany them on the trip. The princess and the captain have known Tuck for decades. Tell them about it, Tuck."

"I just couldn't pass up a free vacation," Tuck said with a shrug.

"Congratulations, Tuck!" Doc exclaimed and clapped. "Have a blast!"

"So we're providing added security for Tuck's sake," Louis concluded.

"Partly," the president replied. "That's where it gets sticky."

"Here it comes," Q said softly.

"We're at our best on 'sticky' missions," Doc quickly replied. "Do we at least have a particular enemy on our radar?"

"I've saved the best for last," the president said. "Recently, INTERPOL intercepted a text message sent by a suspected member of a new Chinese underground extremist group that calls itself Zhēngfú. They advocate China's world domination by any means necessary."

"Zhēngfú," Doc repeated. "Never heard of them. What's it mean?"

"Conquest," the president said flatly. "Intelligence circles have code-named them 'Red

Z.'They meet in members' homes and are reportedly threatening deadly bombings around Beijing. The intercepted text message hinted at plans to hijack the *Dragon* ... which we assume means they plan to hold the Princess Royal hostage as well."

"A twofer!" Q observed in his own special way.

"Do we know anything more about them?" Doc asked hopefully.

"Chinese intelligence recently arrested a suspect they claim is linked to a conspiracy to bomb the North Korean consulate in Beijing," the president said.

"So they're bloodthirsty," Doc concluded, "if we can believe Chinese intelligence."

"We believe them," the president confirmed. "And make no mistake. Whether there's an attempt to take the *Dragon* from within or without—or if there is no attempt at all—the potential for treachery will be around every bend of this trip. So this mission will require more from each of you than any before it," the president said solemnly.

"Tuck's safety is paramount, of course," he continued. "He is the only American the Chinese approved to make the trip. And to complicate matters even more, he will need to move about the train freely. It helps that Captain Michaels has known for years that Tuck's a hopeless train addict. The princess is too. Plus, she's making the trip to closely study the practicality of purchasing *Dragon*-class trains to bring Great Britain's aging rail system into the twenty-first century. So she may very well move about the train as much or more than Tuck. And we have no idea whether, and how often, her husband will move around with her."

"So how do we protect them if no other Americans can be onboard?" Doc asked earnestly.

Madeleine and Noah raised a hand simultaneously.

"Noah will be Omar Keller, a sales representative for a Swiss custom sword and cutlery manufacturer," the president revealed. "Meanwhile, Madeleine will be Ariana Marie Russo, a well-to-do femme fatale who has never laid eyes on the handsome Omar until she had the good fortune of winning a ride aboard the *Dragon*'s transcontinental voyage in a regional Italian lottery."

"But the Chinese will use facial recognition scans during boarding," Doc said urgently.

"You'll be happy to know, Doc, that the Chinese are still unaware that you and the team exist," the president advised him. "But in the name of caution, be sure to call them Omar and Ariana on the phone."

"We'll be able to call them securely?" Doc asked.

"I'm getting to that," the president said with a grin. "You, Louis, Jenny, and Q will take positions at key scheduled stops along the route and stay in touch with Noah and

Tuck via these new wrist phones just approved by the NIC," the president said.

"Won't Chinese security intercept our calls?" Louis asked.

"Inside the cars, yes," the president said. "They're pressurized like airliners for sound deadening and comfort at high speeds, and you can bet they're equipped with listening and jamming devices. Passengers will move between cars via comfortable, enclosed connectors. But it's possible to step outside the connectors onto small, open-air platforms. Our intelligence tells us the Reds cut corners on those platforms and have no way of monitoring satellite calls there. But the platforms will be windy, noisy, and exposed to the elements. So make your calls to Doc and the others from there. But make them sparingly … and brief."

"Roger that, Mr. President!" Noah said.

"I've told you everything we're confident of," the president said. "But we know very little about the *Dragon*'s underbelly. The most mysterious and amazing details we lack are how the beast will ride on the various types, ages, and gauges of tracks in each country it passes through and what propels it on those tracks. So Noah and Madeleine, the more information you can provide about all that, the better."

"Every military application the *Dragon* has depends on it being able to cross borders seamlessly. Not surprisingly, their sales pitch promoting the *Dragon* includes an offer to construct a new mag-lev track linking major cities and harbors at no charge. But it will run on existing rails in the meantime. It's a fearsome logistical advantage. The ability to disable it remotely would be invaluable and might be the difference between victory and defeat."

"You make it sound like we're about to go to war," Doc said.

"I don't mean to, Doc," the president assured him. "My administration's pledge has always been—and remains —to do everything within our power to avoid armed conflict. But knowledge is power. And the more knowledge we have, the less likely it will be that our nation will ever go to war again.

"So the team has just one vital task on this mission, Doc: Vigilance. Your special brand of it will help ensure England's Princess Royal and her husband enjoy an uneventful journey without a clue regarding our role in their protection during the trip ... and it might very well help save the free world in the years ahead."

"Did you rehearse that?" Q asked with an impressed expression.

"No, but I did run it through my mind a couple of times earlier this afternoon," the president chuckled. "That's all I have unless you have questions. Going once! Going twice! Gone! Jenny, Louis, and Tuck, I've planned for you to join Melania and me for supper. How's that sound?"

"Wonderful!" Jenny quickly answered.

"Roger that!" Louis agreed.

"Doc, you and everyone else will have to wait until the next time you're in D.C. That's it for now. Be well!" the president said and ended the session.

5

THE PRINCESS AND THE "DRAGON"

T he state-owned China Railway Group had spared no expense producing the promotional video. It dramatically chronicled how the *Dragon* was conceived by Chinese designers and engineers and brought to life by thousands of skilled laborers and craftspeople working around the clock over the past year and a half at a network of high-tech facilities around the Haidian District of Beijing.

Rafe studied the video closely the entire next week. Doc and his team did the same at their compound overlooking Flathead Lake in northern Montana, near the U.S.-Canadian border. After many viewings, they called one another on their secure satellite network and discussed their thoughts and questions regarding the security challenges presented by the *Dragon*'s groundbreaking interior and exterior engineering.

In particular, they brainstormed the potential military

applications of the engineering contained in the *Dragon*'s undercarriage. Though it was the most vital component of the train, it was mentioned only in very vague terms in the video. Still, what they saw and heard in the presentation sparked their imaginations ... and concerns.

"How much of the video can we believe?" Doc asked Tuck.

"I'd say most of it," Tuck replied, "because it will be easy to check once the *Dragon* is unveiled next month."

"So summarize the *Dragon*'s magic," Rafe pressed for details.

"It's groundbreaking!" Tuck marveled. "Instead of having massive engines at the front and rear of the train pulling and pushing the entire train along, each car is separately propelled by a mystifying combination of high-efficiency electromagnetic drive propulsion and electric motors that drive independently suspended wheels. And that's just the beginning."

"Keep going, Tuck," Doc encouraged him. "I want to hear how the *Dragon* is going to navigate over two continents' worth of mountains, valleys, deserts, and plains, from one nation to the next on tracks that will vary from 1,400 millimeters to 750 millimeters wide. It's hard to believe that can be done at all, let alone at high speed."

"The engineering details are top secret, of course. But

what little the video reveals about the *Dragon*'s navigation system suggests that a series of lasers and motion sensors in its nose adjust the train's undercarriage to the rails beneath it, while they also scan and assess the condition and gauge of the rails up to a half-mile ahead. It collects the data regardless of weather conditions and feeds it to onboard computers, which somehow make the required adjustments to the train's speed and attitude in order to ensure its wheels are at the correct width and angle for the safest, fastest, quietest, and smoothest ride possible."

"You make it sound highly desirable and perfectly harmless," Rafe noted. "So what is it that makes the *Dragon* vulnerable … and dangerous?"

"For starters, if the laser system gets damaged, the *Dragon* would effectively be blind and likely come to a complete stop automatically," Tuck conjectured. "That wouldn't benefit hijackers because the train would literally be dead in its tracks, and there would very likely be nothing the crew or anyone else could do to restart it.

"However," Tuck continued, "if terrorists manage to hack the onboard computers prior to, or during, the trip, the *Dragon* and its passengers would be at their mercy. A group like the Red Z could bring the train to a halt, redirect it, or—in a worst-case scenario— accelerate the train to 500 miles per hour and derail it practically at will."

"Oh, is that all?" Rafe chimed in with an attempt to lighten the conversation.

"No, unfortunately, it's not," Tuck replied ominously. "In fact, I fear that's not at all the worst possible scenario."

"Whoa! Slow down, Tuck!" Doc interrupted. "The military strategist in you is moving too fast for me to keep up. Pretend you're talking to a fifth-grader."

"Okay, let's set aside the possibility of a hijacking for a moment," Tuck suggested. "Let's assume the trip goes exactly as planned without a major hitch or even a minor hiccup."

"Our job is finished, and we can all go home!" Rafe cheered happily.

"For a little while," Tuck said in his most ominous tone yet.

"What are you suggesting, Tuck?" Doc sighed in frustration.

"Chinese strategists always take the long view," Tuck explained. "Decision-makers in the West occupy themselves with five- or ten-year plans—while their Sino counterparts think in terms of a generation or more."

"So what?" Rafe asked dismissively.

"China could gain enormous strategic military advantages by laying groundwork that's practically invisible to outsiders blinded by shorter-term thinking. So, for instance, the Chinese government will leverage the *Dragon's* maiden journey to sell the groundbreaking high-speed train and its advanced combination mag-lev/rail system to nations from one end of the European and Asian continents to the other," Tuck continued.

"Meanwhile, Chinese military strategists will no doubt use the transcontinental voyage to woo nations like Turkey, Bulgaria, and even the United Kingdom into welcoming the very system that could one day carry China's own high-speed trains loaded with military hardware and troops to distant wartime fronts."

"If I didn't know better, I'd say you were paranoid," Doc told him. "But it all makes sense. So the reality is that while we help ensure nothing goes wrong on this trip, its success could be just as dangerous to the entire world in the long run."

"Yet still another possibility will make it hard to sleep the next three weeks: Everything I've told you could merely be the product of my overactive imagination, and I'm needlessly frightening everyone responsible for protecting what will ultimately be a peaceful trip."

"Whatever the case," Doc declared, "it's important for the team and the president to hear and consider everything you've just laid out for us, Tuck. I believe you've captured the filter through which we should process everything we hear and observe during the trip."

"Agreed," Tuck replied. "And we've got approximately two weeks to think through all we know and believe about the *Dragon* before China informs the world media of the trip."

"Once that happens," Doc added, "you just gotta know the media will spin fantastical coverage with themes like 'the Princess and the *Dragon*.' The train will take on a life of its own. News and feature coverage will be filled with speculation and misinformation. Between now and then, the team needs to focus on understanding what *we* know and believe about the *Dragon* to ensure we're on course before the rest of the world runs wild with excitement about what will be a global media spectacle.

"Tuck, make sure the president hears all that you just told us," Doc said. "We also need to advise the rest of the team and then begin familiarizing ourselves with the comfort and luxury aboard the *Dragon*. And finally, we'll need to brainstorm how the team onboard and off can be most effective while remaining invisible. So view the video at least one more time tonight with that in mind, and we'll convene the whole team at 0800 hours tomorrow. That's 0200 hours for you, Rafe. So turn in early!"

"Don't worry about me, Doc!" Rafe replied. "For legionnaires, sleep is a luxury!"

Connie awoke a little before six the next morning and quickly showered before preheating the oven for the biscuits and cinnamon rolls she promised Q she would have waiting for him. When the first batch was in the oven, she poured herself a cup of coffee and moved to the living room of the big lake house to get a look at the morning mist rising off Flathead Lake as the sun came up over the mountains to the east. She was surprised to see Q sitting in a rocker on the front porch with his legs crossed at the ankles, and his wide-brim Stetson pulled down over his eyes. He hadn't bothered to hitch Montana to the porch railing because he knew the big Appaloosa would be content to graze on the sweet, wet grass in the front yard.

"Morning, Q!" Connie said cheerfully through a front window. "Coffee's ready, and you look like you could use some. Sound good?"

"Sounds wonderful!" Q said and pushed the brim of the Stetson up off his eyes with a forefinger while his lips formed a sleepy smile.

"I'll be right back with one as soon as I get the first batch of biscuits out of the oven and slide the next batch in," Connie told him sweetly.

"Montana, you don't know what you're missin'," Q said softly and breathed in the welcome aroma of fresh-baked biscuits.

"Coffee, cream, sugar, biscuits, butter, jam, and honey," Connie recited happily and set a tray-full on a small table beside Q's rocker.

"Now I know why I woke up so early and couldn't go back to sleep," Q mumbled as he prepped his coffee and chose his first biscuit.

Connie sat in the closest of the three remaining rockers and sipped her coffee.

"Will we see Marsha this morning?" she asked her husband's best friend.

"That would be my guess," Q said and took his first sip. "This meeting's likely to be a long one, and she'll come looking for me to go into town with her for one reason or another."

"And you'll be grateful," Connie chuckled.

"That I will," Q agreed softly as he surveyed Flathead Lake stretched out before them.

"When are you going to admit that you love these meetings, Q?" Doc asked as he stepped out onto the porch holding a large mug of coffee. "And Connie, if you keep giving this man fresh-baked biscuits, we'll never be rid of him."

"I keep coming back for your warm welcomes, not the biscuits!" Q shot back.

The rest of the team arrived in the next few minutes, and everyone gathered around the dining room table for light conversation with coffee, biscuits, and cinnamon rolls before they moved to the safe room in the basement and got down to business.

"Okay, you've all reviewed your copies of the video," Doc began. "So I know you have thoughts and questions. Let's start by discussing your thoughts."

"It's amazing!" Jenny blurted out. "I'd love to be going!"

"Why, exactly?" Doc prodded her.

"It's beautiful!" she gushed. "I mean, from the upholstery to the draperies, the wall coverings, the art, carpeting, and color choices are just perfect. It looks so roomy and comfortable. I initially thought spending eight or more days aboard a train would be torture. But now I feel more like it would be the next best thing to an ocean cruise!"

"The deluxe compartments *do* look roomy and comfortable," Madeleine agreed. "I'm sure I'll feel cozy and secure in mine. And if it's as quiet as the video claims, I'll have plenty of time to catch up on my sleep."

"I was surprised that they bragged about the room service," Noah added. "I assumed passengers would be encouraged to mingle in the dining cars. But the video stressed the option of private dining in your compartment to enjoy a meal alone or with another passenger."

"It's important to remember that *this Dragon* is one of a kind," Doc told them. "The interior was crafted to showcase China's engineering, innovation, and rider services. It's a celebration of their nation's ability to provide the world's safest, most luxurious high-speed rail travel. It's quite different from the version China will provide its citizens and sell to the world.

"That said, let's talk about the compartments Madeleine, Noah, and Tuck will occupy during the trip," Doc said.

"I'm impressed with the privacy and comfort my compartment appears to provide," Madeleine said. "There's a comfy chair and reading lamp, a small table to dine at if I like, a sofa large enough for two adults, a thirty-inch flat-screen with a Blu-ray player—plus a roomy bed, blackout shades, and lots of storage space. And my own roomy bathroom and shower are the icing on the cake!"

"The Chinese seem to have gone to a great deal of trouble and expense and even used gender-specific fabrics and color schemes. Mine has dark wood paneling, navy-blue upholstery, and brass hardware and fixtures."

"Mine does, too," Tuck added.

"My walls and furniture are covered with plush, pastel fabrics, and the hardware and fixtures are trimmed with Mother of Pearl," Madeleine said.

"I simply *must* get a ticket on that train!" Jenny gushed.

"The *Dragon* has its own phone network with a phone in each compartment, correct?" Doc asked to be sure.

"Correct!" Madeleine confirmed. "But of course, it's tapped."

"You can count on it," Q chimed in.

"You shouldn't call one another anyway," Doc reminded them. "Remember, you're all strangers. Only use your encrypted watch-phones to contact a team member on board or off … and always call from a platform between cars. Now let's talk about the rest of the train."

"The three dining cars are large and spectacular," Madeleine said. "They're similar to dining rooms aboard cruise liners, not at all like I would have imagined."

"And the open seating will make it easy for you to circulate and interact with just about any other passengers you feel is necessary," Doc noted. "So make it a point to always sit at a different table for each meal."

"The sample menu in the video is quite remarkable," Tuck said. "I hope it's accurate."

"And there will be live music during supper!" Madeleine added. "How romantic is that?"

"Madeleine, I do believe you're getting into the spirit of your character," Doc chuckled.

"Let's hope I can get her back out of it after the trip," Noah said with a hearty laugh.

"I only have eyes for you, baby!" Madeleine gushed and squeezed her husband's hand.

"You two are an inspiration!" Connie said.

"Let's talk about the rest of the train's layout," Doc said. "We know there'll be at least forty-five cars, each more than 100 feet long. Three of them will be combination dining and observation cars. Two galley cars are sandwiched between them. Two more contain office space and living quarters for the crew and security personnel. One is right behind the lead car, the other is between the princess's car and the rear lead car."

"What the hell is a 'rear lead car'?" Q asked.

"Well, Q," Doc pointedly replied, "if you had paid closer attention to the video, you would have realized that, unlike conventional trains, the cars in the front and back are not engines. The engines are located beneath each car. So the cars at either end are called 'lead cars' because the crew controls the train from one or the other, depending on which way the train is going."

"Got it!" Q simply replied.

"Then there's a lounge car with an observation deck above it near the front of the train, and another for smokers near the rear," Doc added. "There will also be a car containing an infirmary with accommodations for a physician and a second car to accommodate his staff. That's sixteen cars accounted for. I'll let Noah, Madeleine, and Tuck tell us what they're thinking regarding the remaining cars."

"You go first, Madeleine," Noah told his wife softly.

"Well … I'll tell you what little I know—and what I've imagined—about the royal cars," she quietly began. "For starters, the princess and her husband each have a separate car at the rear of the train, just before what Doc likes to call 'the rear lead car.' And from what we can tell with only the brief glimpse given in the video, I'd say both cars are over the top in terms of comfort, luxury, and space. Princess Mary must love lavender and velvet because they're everywhere you look in her car."

"Those were two of her favorites when I first met her years ago," Tuck confirmed. "Apparently, they still are."

"Apparently," Madeleine echoed. "She enters the car through a beautifully appointed living room-type space with an extremely realistic fireplace, nicely framed prints of paintings by British artists, and lots of Queen Anne furniture. If you go to the left, moving forward in the car, there's a small library/study. Beyond that is a cozy sitting area/sleeping compartment with a private bath for the princess's personal assistant. To the right of the living room, moving rearward in the car, is a small, modern kitchenette, then a wardrobe room, and finally a large bedroom with a king-size, four-poster bed and a gorgeous, large bathroom.

"The captain's car is laid out much the same, but he doesn't travel with a personal assistant, which gives him even more room. Tuck's is likely the mirror image as he's the personal guest of the royal couple."

"I doubt it's any more *special* than yours and Noah's,

Madeleine," Tuck said from his chair in a room off the Situation Room under the Oval. "And I am quite happy with it, thank you. What *is* special is that it's in the tail end of the rear security car, which will accommodate a half-dozen or so officers of England's Royalty Protection Command. They—and I—will be just before Marty's—eh, Captain Michaels's car. The princess's car will be just behind it, followed by the rear lead car, which I would guess will always have two or more security officers riding there.

"While that could make it awkward for me to slip out onto a platform unnoticed when I need to make calls, I should have a great view of both the Chinese and British officers' movements," Tuck reasoned.

"You bet it will," Doc agreed. "Now, unless there are any other questions about the cars, I'd like to move on to a few puzzling questions I have about this mission."

"Let's hear 'em," Tuck said.

"First of all, where did this *Dragon* come from so suddenly?" Doc began

"I'm glad you asked," Tuck said with a squint. "I'm wondering the same thing."

"I hoped you would ask that, Tuck," Doc said softly. "The only thing remotely close to the *Dragon* that I've experienced is a mag-lev prototype Beijing unveiled more than three years ago when it announced a plan to use it to ferry tourists between downtown Shanghai and the Shanghai Pudong International Airport."

"That's the only one I knew of, as well, until now," Tuck confirmed. "It was supposed to travel at about 230 miles per hour and cut the commute time from an hour to seven minutes. And frankly, that's the last anyone in the West heard of it, which is what kept it off our Defense Department's radar."

"So we were caught with our pants around our ankles when the Reds rolled out a high-tech beast that travels along any gauge track, or no track at all, at speeds approaching 500 miles per hour," Doc told the team. "And now we're scrambling to assess the monster's potential military applications. What the hell has the CIA been doing the past year and a half?"

"Frankly, I don't know what the president's heard about this during his daily briefings," Tuck replied. "But I didn't hear a thing about it from him until I received my invitation to take the trip. And now that I've resigned, I don't have any idea how much he'll tell me."

"You resigned?!" Doc asked in disbelief. "When?"

"Unofficially, last week, before my invitation arrived," Tuck said matter-of-factly. "I thought the whole world knew. It seems to be the president's angle to comply with China's prohibition of U.S. political figures aboard the *Dragon* during this trip. I must admit that being invited by the royal couple is a pretty good cover. So I can hardly blame him for using it."

"Whatever made it possible, I'm glad to have you on the team for this mission, Tuck," Doc assured him. "Having your eyes and instincts on board the train will serve us well. So will your knowledge and experience with Princess Mary. What can you tell me about her? How is it that a woman the world barely knows just might find herself at the center of a deadlier drama than Helen of Troy?"

"Well, unlike Helen, she's no beauty," Tuck said with a wry grin. "But she's easy to like and hard to forget. Her smile and laugh are infectious. She's approachable and genuine, two qualities that are as surprising as they are refreshing, given her station. She loves traveling and meeting new people. And she's been a lover of trains since childhood.

"It's no coincidence that China offered her this trip," Tuck said flatly. "They did their homework and made her an offer they knew she couldn't resist. Their invitation to experience the *Dragon* tapped into every one of her passions: A romantic train adventure across two continents with dozens of foreign strangers to befriend—and the potential to bring the British rail system into the twenty-first century."

"Sounds like a major win-win proposition in a perfect world," Doc replied. "But we're stuck in this world, with all its dangers. It's ironic that the princess will be at the center of this intrigue as she heads home, while Homer's Helen was forcefully dragged off to Troy."

"Yeah," Tuck sighed. "Let's just hope truth isn't stranger than fiction on this mission."

"Let me warn you, Tuck," Doc said with a tense grin, "that would make it an exception."

"Well, come what may, it's an honor to work with you and the rest of the team, Doc," Tuck replied. "I'll give it my absolute best."

"I know you will, Captain," Doc said with a hand on Tuck's shoulder. "I know you will."

6

RED Z RISING

The *Beijing News's* midmorning edition headline screamed a single word in three languages: "征服 *Zhēngfú! Conquest!*" The secondary headline shouted, *"Terrorists Massacre 307 Innocents!"* The state-owned newspaper wanted to ensure everyone knew the name of the savage underground mob that had claimed responsibility for the deadly blast on a busy platform at Beijing's South Railway Station. Area hospitals were overwhelmed with more than 500 seriously injured commuters.

News of the rail station bombing broke too late that morning to save employees from bomb blasts at three Beijing branches of the Industrial and Commercial Bank of China. Those blasts killed 137 and gravely injured 248 others. According to the Beijing Public Security Bureau, surveillance videos revealed the simultaneous explosions were caused by improvised

devices in briefcases left on chairs in the banks' huge
lobbies as employees arrived for work.

At 9 a.m. Beijing time (8 p.m. the prior evening in
Washington D.C.), the rest of the world got its first look
at the death and destruction unleashed by Zhēngfú.
President Prescott and his chief of staff, Jasper
Cornwall, watched videotaped coverage of the
barbarian attacks in the Situation Room. Doc and the
rest of the President's Dozen took in the sight as they
stood holographically in the center of the room.
Meanwhile, Tuck was speechless on a secure phone line
while he watched TV coverage at his home.

"Well, the Red Z has declared war," Cornwall said softly
to the president while hardly able to blink. "But against
whom? Did the CIA have any warning this could
happen?"

"If so, they didn't share it with me," the president sighed.

"So we have no clue whether this bunch has plans for
more of the same—or worse—inside or outside of
China?" Doc asked. "Say, for instance, onboard the
Dragon?"

"Afraid not," Cornwall softly replied. "But there are
reports of having heard people shouting 'zuìzhōng de
zhēngfú' seconds before the train station bombing."

"What the hell does that mean?" Q growled.

"The Ultimate Victory," Cornwall told him. "Which they
are obviously still very far from achieving."

"Armstrong and Reed are on the way over," the president said. "Let's head upstairs. But I don't want to share our level of concern about this with them just yet. Let's see what they have to say first. Hopefully, they have something they should have shared before now. Tuck, stay on the line. Doc, we're muting your line while Armstrong and Reed are in the Oval."

"Roger that!" Doc shot back.

CIA Director Brett Reed and Elaine Armstrong, the president's director of National Intelligence, were both slightly winded when they entered the Oval.

"Welcome!" the president boomed from his chair. "We have to stop meeting like this."

"Tell that to the Reds," Reed replied, shaking his head as he and Armstrong took seats.

"I will," the president answered. "But first, how about telling me what the hell is going on in Beijing?"

"Intel on this is still pretty fuzzy, Mr. President," Armstrong said. "We're both inclined to believe the Chinese government saw something like this coming."

"So you're saying they let it happen?" the president asked incredulously.

"We can't be sure," Reed interrupted. "But normally, they would step up security measures in public places following the intel we believe they have on this bunch. At the very least, the rumored plot to blow up the

North Korean embassy should have put Beijing on high alert."

"But it didn't?" the president asked even more incredulously.

"Not according to our sources," Armstrong replied.

"Perhaps the government didn't take the plot seriously," the president suggested.

"They take all such plots seriously," Reed assured him.

"So what are you saying?" The president pressed for facts.

"There have been rumblings in and around Beijing over the past several weeks that lead us to suspect Red Z is sponsored in whole or in part by a cell inside the government," Reed said.

"So you're telling me it appears the Reds may have maimed and murdered their own citizens?" the president asked as he rubbed his brow. "Why would they do that?"

"Attacks like these could set the stage for a new government crackdown," Armstrong asserted. "It also lends a lot of weight to the public perception that the regime is under increasingly violent pressures to adopt a more aggressive global expansionist policy."

"Every government is under all kinds of pressures, Brett," the president said. "Why manufacture more?"

"Possibly to appear more moderate than is actually the case and tip the scales of public opinion in the regime's favor," Reed added.

"This all raises interesting questions," the president told them as he rose from his chair and leaned forward with his fists resting on the Resolute.

Cornwall recognized the president's body language and braced for the barrage to come.

"But we need answers, damn it! What the hell is going on over there?! Are you telling me we don't have even one asset on the ground who can help us understand this?"

"Zhongnanhai isn't as porous as D.C., Mr. President," Armstrong said carefully. "The Reds forbid freedom of speech for a reason."

"Bullshit!" the president shot back at her. "You know better than I that China has citizens who treasure liberty as much as we do! And if that isn't a powerful enough motivation, greed sure as hell is! But you're tellin' me we haven't even been able to *buy* the answers we need?

"I need answers, damn it!" the president said firmly. "And here are a few more questions. First, how in the hell did China transform a carnival ride into the world's fastest, land-based military machine in less than two years without our having a clue that they were doing it? Second, what do the terrorists know about the *Dragon* that we don't? Finally—and most important—what's the

Dragon's weakest link? And where is it most likely to be attacked?

"And just for the sake of my blood pressure, I need to understand how the Reds managed to attract zero attention while they secretly conducted 500 mile-per-hour test runs. Our satellites should have accidentally seen it, for Christ's sake!" the president practically shouted. "We'll have an American and other assets on board that monster when it leaves Shanghai. Their mission is to ensure England's Princess Mary and her husband return home from their trip safe and sound. Our mission is to bring our team home in the same shape they left in, or better. Understood?" he asked as he stood to send Armstrong and Reed on their way.

"Understood!" Armstrong answered for both of them as they turned to leave.

"With the answers you collect, plus a little luck and God's grace, our team will return with selfies and happy stories," the president said as he led them to the door.

Cornwall let out a long, deep breath as the pair exited the Oval, and the president headed back to his desk with an intent look.

"I think they got the message," he told the president.

"I sure as hell hope so," the president replied. "I won't suffer through another meeting like this one, Jasper. Start pulling files of prospective replacements."

"Will do, Mr. President," Jasper said. "I'll have them on your desk early tomorrow."

"Doc, are you still on the line?" the president boomed as he unmuted the secure line.

"Sure am, Mr. President," Doc chuckled. "Who could fall asleep during that train wreck? Besides, I think I have some of the answers you're looking for."

"I'm all ears!" the president huffed, still fuming about the two he'd just sent away.

"Connie and I spent two weeks in Shanghai and Ningbo last year, and I believe the *Dragon* was tested on the Shanghai to Shanghai Pao Airport shuttle loop at night," Doc began.

"Tell me more," the president prodded.

"The track is a little over thirty-five miles long, and the popular mag-lev train travels station to station in under eight minutes," Doc told him. "It's a great ride. If there were no windows, passengers would never guess how fast it moves. The ride's unbelievably smooth and quiet, and a huge improvement over the hour-plus it takes to drive from Shanghai to the airport."

"And …?" the president pressed for a point to be made.

"The train performed perfectly," Doc explained. "The flow of travelers is endless between Shanghai and the airport. But no one could tell Connie and I why the train didn't run after dark. All anyone would tell us was that no trains had run between 6 p.m. and 5 a.m. for the past couple of months, and no one was sure when nighttime service would resume."

"So you're saying they tested the train under the dark of night?" the president asked.

"That would be my guess," Doc tossed back at the president. "Test runs at 400 to 500 miles an hour could make round trips in ten or eleven minutes and would make almost no noise."

"That's still far from ideal conditions," Cornwall suggested. "Testing the viability and reliability of a 500-mile-per-hour train would require sustained runs of at least 100 miles."

"You're probably right, Jasper," Doc agreed. "But the airport corridor was obviously a viable option to support initial development while the government constructed another 1,000 miles of elevated track between Shanghai and Chongqing. That provided an ever-growing nighttime track over the past two years. Meanwhile, they could have constructed a circular, hundred-mile-long test track underground for around-the-clock runs anywhere along the route. A 100-mile loop would require a complex about thirty-five miles in diameter."

"Beijing could pull it off," the president said. "But the cost would be astronomical."

"True, but the return on investment would have been total secrecy," Doc countered. "And that's China's M.O."

"Granted," the president conceded. "But knowing how the *Dragon* was created doesn't tell us anything about its weaknesses."

"That's one of the obvious benefits China got from complete secrecy," Doc reasoned. "As for weaknesses, I think the most obvious is the same as it is for all trains: the track. And Red Z appears to be proficient in IEDs."

"It's a nightmare to think that they simply have to plant one or more devices of sufficient shape and size anywhere along the thousands of miles of track the *Dragon* will travel and wait for it to come to them," Cornwall said. "There are stretches of track, especially outside of China, where the *Dragon* may as well be on the far side of the moon. There's no way in the world anyone can secure the entire route, no matter how far in advance it's announced."

"The worst nightmare in all this is not knowing Red Z's objective," the president said. "If it's money and publicity, they could disable the *Dragon* and hold it, the princess, and everyone else aboard hostage. If they want to trigger an international conflict, they could blow the *Dragon* up and make it appear to be the work of an innocent nation. Until we know more, the list of possible scenarios is almost endless, Doc. So we have little hope of understanding the intrigue that surrounds this venture before it begins … which is why I'm counting on your team to uncover and thwart any threats that emerge as the *Dragon* makes the journey."

"Once again, it looks like we'll need to make it up as we go," Doc said. "You can count on us, Mr. President," Doc said.

"I know I can, Doc, and I'm grateful," the president said, and ended the call.

After the call, Doc and his team gathered around the oak table in his safe room. Tuck and Rafe were on secure lines, and together, they processed what little they knew.

"Well, Doc," Q said, "if we're not in over our heads, we're at least up to our chins. How do we protect a moving train up to 500 miles per hour through at least twelve countries?"

Doc looked around the table at the team he trusted with his life before responding.

"Well, the negatives are obvious," he said. "Let's start chipping away at the positives."

"I think it will help that we'll have some of us on the train and the rest off," Madeleine said. "How, exactly, I'm not sure. But it seems better than having us all on or all off."

"And if all goes according to plan, we'll be able to contact one another whether we're on or off the train," Noah said.

"We'll be on the ground, not 35,000 feet in the air – and on a track or rails the entire trip," Jenny added. "So we don't have to worry about a sudden loss of cabin pressure or simply vanishing as we know can happen to airliners."

"We'll have allies and security on board," Noah noted. "Hopefully, *everyone* aboard will want to reach London safely. At worst, I imagine only one or two could have other plans."

"Unfortunately, that last positive presents us with the fly in the ointment," Doc noted.

"And the monkey in the wrench, to quote John McClain," Q chimed in.

"John who?" Noah asked.

"John McClain!" Q shot back in surprise. "*Die Hard*! You've never seen the movie?"

"Afraid not," Noah admitted.

"I've got the DVD," Q told him. "Come over tonight, and we'll watch it. You'll love it."

"I hate to interrupt," Doc said pointedly. "But can we get back to work, now?"

"Sorry, Doc," Q replied sincerely. "Noah just caught me off guard."

"Focus, Q," Doc shot back.

"I believe President Prescott's correct," Tuck said over the phone. "Red Z is on the rise, and the *Dragon* is a logical target. If they make their way aboard on this trip, we must find them as quickly and quietly as possible. That challenge alone is monumental because I believe they'll remain in hiding while the *Dragon* is in China."

"Why do you think that, Tuck?" Doc asked with spiked interest.

"They've already struck a major blow at the heart of their homeland with the Beijing bombings," Tuck explained. "They've demonstrated that they're a force to be reckoned with. But they've made neither threats nor demands and issued no manifesto. That's not normal. If it's true they advocate China's domination of the world, how do they envision that happening? How do they intend to help make it happen?"

"What's your best guess?" Doc asked hopefully.

"I have none," Tuck said with frustration. "I don't believe anyone does. Not the CIA. Not INTERPOL. And worst of all, I don't think Beijing has a clue, either."

"Maybe this Red Z isn't a threat to the *Dragon* at all," Q suggested.

"Quite the opposite," Tuck responded quickly. "The *Dragon* is not only a logical target. It's a perfect detonator for global conflict. Blowing it up or seizing it along with the princess and the rest of the passengers would capture the world's attention. And if the terrorists don't take credit for the attack, rumors, theories, and old hatreds would run wild. I can't think of a better way to trigger a world war, short of bombing the United Nations headquarters in New York."

"What does all this add up to?" Louis asked the question that was on everyone's mind.

"We're flying by the seat of our pants," Doc said and looked around the table again.

"On a train instead of an airplane," Q added in exasperation.

"We haven't heard a word from you, Rafe," Doc said to the former legionnaire, who was listening intently on his secure line. "What's running through that warrior mind of yours?"

"Land mines," Rafe said simply.

"Land mines?" Doc echoed to be sure he heard the Frenchman right.

"If they show up, there will only be a few of them. So they'll be positioned strategically, and it will be hard to find them until they lash out where we least expect them," Rafe explained.

"Like land mines," Doc said quietly.

"Exactly," Rafe replied. "So while we list possible ambush sites, we must look very closely at sites that seem unlikely at first glance."

"Gimme your top three candidates," Doc prompted him.

"The first is the point of departure, Shanghai's

Hongqiao Railway Station, because it makes no obvious sense to scuttle the trip before it begins ... and precisely where the Chinese government could mount the most potent response.

"Next, I'd take a close, hard look at the Qinghai Tibet Railway, the highest in the world. Its Tanggula Station is more than 16,000 meters above sea level. Most passengers require oxygen during much, if not all, of the 550 kilometer stretch of track. The *Dragon* would have to slow to under 100 kilometers per hour to ride the track that's built on unstable permafrost. Attacking along that stretch would be a suicide mission because there's no escape route.

"But the site that worries me the most is the London Waterloo," Rafe said solemnly.

"Scratch that one," his sister blurted out. "It's the end of the line—the heart of London. It'll be jammed with media, British Transport Police, Scotland Yard, and at least a company of the Queen's Guard."

"Exactly!" Rafe insisted. "Waterloo is the absolute least likely place to hijack the train. The day it arrives, all other rail services will be halted. The station will be completely locked down. Security there will be on high alert. Yet, those aboard the *Dragon* are likely to let their guard down. Who would blame them after guarding against the worst around the clock for a week and a half?

"With the world watching, a threat to blow up the

Dragon and kidnap or kill the princess would spark bedlam around the globe. Red Z would be at the control of an international drama. They could shake down every nation with citizens on board. No demand would be too great. No price would be too high. But the nightmare is that money may not be enough … if their ultimate objective is World War III."

7

RETURN OF A HERO

L a Santé Prison looms like an old ghost near the heart of Paris. Built in 1867 with 500 cells, the number grew to 1,000 by 1900. Known of late as the "VIP Prison," its flashy nickname belies the stark walls, dark halls, and stained concrete floors within. A well-publicized five-year effort to renovate the labyrinth of corroding stone and steel began in 2014, but few signs of success were yet visible within its walls. Not that it matters to the men who were locked inside, awaiting execution.

Within a dank quarter, oddly dubbed the "Special Section," La Santé's newest man with no hope stared silently into the darkness of his cell, squatted deep atop his shoeless feet and leaned back against a cold cement wall opposite his stainless steel cot, with its eight-inch legs welded to one-inch bolts that were lagged deep into the floor. Despite the harsh conditions, the media gave it the "VIP" label when headline-grabbing butchers like the Panamanian dictator and drug lord Manuel Noriega and the Venezuelan terrorist, Carlos the Jackal, were briefly confined there. But Chastain was no butcher. He was France's most decorated and celebrated hero, to whom it had awarded its Legion of Honor for single-handedly foiling a plot to assassinate President Jacques DuPris.

Now, the once-chiseled, 6'4" inch, 240-pound warrior struggled with PTSD and a serious brain injury that surfaced long after he'd received it while fighting for the nation he loved. That's when Chastain's behavior became bizarrely erratic, and he believed himself to be the sixteenth-century seer, Nostradamus, with a mission to save President DuPris from another planned assassination plot he "foretold" in a journal of predictions he called his scrolls. When Chastain briefly ran wild in the U.S. while AWOL from the legion two years earlier, Doc only half-kiddingly told Q the French people thought of their hero as the Lone Ranger, G.I. Joe, and Superman rolled into one.

It was Rafe who traveled to the U.S., tracked down Chastain, and returned him to France, believing his fellow legionnaire and closest friend would be treated compassionately and receive the medical and psychological care he so desperately needed. But soon after landing in Paris, Chastain learned he was a suspect in a murder investigation, which made him a fugitive as well as a troubled AWOL Legionnaire. Prosecutors clashed over who would try him first, and Chastain was quickly caught up in the voracious gears of so-called civilian and military justice.

So into La Santé's Special Section he went and languished there while the memory of his heroic exploits faded from the public's mind. With only minimal medical treatment and no real psychological support, he soon spiraled downward, sometimes frozen for hours in his cramped squatting position, and stared blankly into the darkest corner of his 10' x 8' cell.

On the afternoon that his friend, Rafe, was on the phone to Doc and the rest of the President's Dozen, a guard slid open the tiny hatch at the bottom of Chastain's cell door and pushed a shallow tin of cold mush and a stale croissant along the floor in his direction. The prisoner stretched out with his belly to the cement and rested on his elbows as he shoved the mush into his mouth with two fingers. In that position, his head was near the trap door, and he realized the guard hadn't closed it fully. Through the opening, with his ears close to the floor, Chastain heard most of a conversation between two guards who stood in front of the next cell.

"Did you hear that court-martialed legionnaire, Bellarose, might be reinstated into the legion?" one said to the other.

"You're kidding, right?" the other replied.

"Nope!" the first said. "I heard he's been given a chance to redeem himself after beating a fellow officer within an inch of his life for making a nasty remark about our boy, Chastain."

"How the hell is he going to do that?" the other asked in disbelief. "You and I would never get a second chance. Why should he?"

"I don't know," the first replied. "But I sure as hell hope it won't be easy for him. If it were up to me, he'd have to agree to a suicide mission. Yes sir. It would have to be a do or die proposition, alright."

Chastain suddenly sat bolt-upright, and his mind began to race.

Rafe was court-martialed? he silently asked his panicked mind. *But why? He tracked me down in the States and risked his life to save mine and tried to get me help when the rest of France wanted my head in a guillotine! I've got to help him! I must get out of here!*

Chastain's heart began to race, and he felt the blood throb within the veins in his neck. He silently rose to his feet and stood at attention in the center of his cell as his mind spun out of control. Standing like a statue, Chastain slipped into a trance like those he'd experienced in America. As the trance deepened, his eyes rolled back in his head, then suddenly opened wide and looked straight ahead. There he stood until a guard peered into his cell and discovered his state. The guard punched the *Medical Emergency* icon on his cell phone and rushed into Chastain's cell with his matraque in hand.

"Chastain! Chastain! Can you hear me?" the guard shouted, but detected no sign of consciousness in the man who was frozen still with his lifeless eyes wide open. "I need help in here now!" the guard yelled as he jabbed his matraque into Chastain's chest but got no reaction.

Two more guards rushed into the cell and saw the first guard strike Chastain behind the knees with his matraque. The blow would tumble a normal man. But Chastain was unfazed.

"What the hell's wrong with him?" one of the guards grunted loudly.

"Don't know," the first said as the three of them circled Chastain. "But it's not good."

"What should we do?" another asked helplessly.

"Stand your ground," the first said resolutely. "Dubois will be here in seconds."

Doctor Dubois breathlessly entered the cell at that very moment and circled Chastain and the guards twice before saying a word. Two brutish-looking orderlies appeared next with a gurney ready in case it was needed and combat training in case Chastain was faking.

"What did you observe before I arrived?" Dubois asked while he pointed a penlight directly into Chastain's vacant eyes and held it within an inch of each pupil.

Dubois was startled when he saw absolutely no dilation

of Chastain's wide-open eyes in reaction to the bright light. There should have at least been some, even in the case of a drug overdose. Dubois next checked Chastain's pulse with a firm squeeze of his wrist. That move also startled the doctor when he realized he was unable to manipulate Chastain's arm or wrist, which were cold to the touch and felt as though rigor mortis had begun.

"Strap him in and get him to the infirmary now!" Dubois commanded the orderlies. "I think he has a brain hemorrhage, and I don't want to have to account for a dead hero!"

The muscular pair were shocked to find that lifting Chastain was like loading a statue onto the gurney. His body was rigid, as though he'd been dead for hours … standing up.

"Hurry!" Dubois shouted as he bolted out of the cell and sprinted in the direction of the infirmary, which was just inside the prison's main gate.

Pretending to be unconscious, the prisoner watched closely as Dubois used a remote to open gates along the route to the examination room.

Yes, hurry, the prisoner silently agreed in his traumatized brain, which was once again flooded with the thoughts of a madman. *I must escape so that I can repay the evil one who tracked me down in America … and make him wish he'd never met the great Nostradamus!*

When Dubois rushed into the infirmary, he reflexively turned on the bright, overhead light above the examination table with one hand and activated the oxygen machine beside the table with the other.

"Get him on the table, quick!" he barked at the orderlies.

The trio knew the man on the gurney was stiff and had no detectable pulse or reflexes. They thought he was dead or dying. But his mind was hyper-alert, and his strength had tripled on the way to the examination room. They thought they were fighting to save Gabriel Chastain's life. But they were about to make the horrible discovery that they must fight to save their own lives because they had come face-to-face with the madman who called himself Nostradamus.

Dubois and the orderlies were not prepared for the fury Nostradamus unleashed in that examination room. He snapped the straps on the gurney like they were crepe paper. They rushed him just as they had been trained. But all three were sent crashing into the cement walls by a superhuman sweep of the madman's left arm. Nostradamus saw Dubois activate the emergency response device that hung from a lanyard around his neck. He knew guards would respond in seconds. One of the orderlies drew a snub-nosed Smith & Wesson from an ankle holster. But Nostradamus kicked it out of his hand and across the room. Then he picked the poor man up by the collar with one hand and slammed him onto the gurney.

Just then, three guards burst into the examination room and crouched with guns drawn.

"Drop your weapons, or I'll crush his windpipe!" Nostradamus growled at them and clutched the orderly's throat in his iron grip.

"What'll we do?" one guard desperately asked the other two.

"Drop 'em!" Nostradamus shouted and squeezed his captive's throat so tightly the man writhed in pain and kicked his legs wildly. "Or he's dead before you get a second shot off!"

Slowly, agonizingly, the guards laid their pistols on the floor.

"Now line up next to the doc!" Nostradamus commanded them. "You got somethin' to knock 'em out?" he asked Dubois.

Dubois reluctantly nodded his head. "Yes."

"Well, do it, or I'll cut their throats!" Nostradamus shouted. "And then I'll cut yours!"

Hands trembling, Dubois retrieved a syringe and a vial of anesthetic from a drawer and injected it into the guards and the orderlies.

"Okay, Doc! Your turn!" Nostradamus said.

Dubois hesitated with fear in his eyes as he watched the others collapse like ragdolls.

"We can do this the easy way ... or the hard way!" Nostradamus said ominously.

The terrified doctor stilled his shaking hands just enough to inject himself, then threw the syringe into a nearby sink and quickly took a seat before the anesthesia took effect.

"No, ya don't!" Nostradamus growled and lifted Dubois out of the chair by the lapels of his lab coat. "You're goin' with me!"

The maniac dropped Dubois onto the gurney and strapped him to it, ripped the lanyard with the gate remote on it from around Dubois's limp neck, then rolled him into the hall in the direction of the main gate. It made no difference to him that guards saw him enter the hall and open the gate. He would be on the street momentarily ... and Dubois was going with him.

"Damn it!" the guard seated at the CCTV shouted at the sight on the screen and punched buttons that activated sirens, emergency lights, and locked the main gate.

But the madman had already wheeled Dubois through it. The guard knew he should have sounded the alarm when Dubois summoned help. He feared he'd lose his job. But he was terrified that Dubois might lose his life ... if he hadn't already.

How thoughtful of them! the madman thought with a maniacal laugh as the heavy main gate automatically closed and locked behind him.

Then he sprinted up Rue de la Santé, rolling the unconscious Dubois along on the gurney by the throat. Traffic stopped at the sight of the two of them, and police sirens grew louder in all directions, but Nostradamus was unfazed. He knew he had a few moments before the police would arrive. He knew that was enough time to reach his destination: the Catacombs of Paris.

When he reached the padlocked entrance, he dumped the unconscious Dubois to the sidewalk, raised the heavy gurney high above his head, and slammed its steel frame down onto the padlock, which shattered and sent pieces flying as far as the middle of the street.

Nostradamus left the still-unconscious Dubois lying half off the curb, his legs sprawled onto Avenue du Général Leclerc, and disappeared inside the nondescript entryway to the nightmarish underground burial grounds the French call the "Empire of Death." Just a few steps in, the madman realized how very dark the passageway was. Then he remembered Dubois's penlight and sprinted back to retrieve it from the doctor's lab coat pocket.

The first police arrived just in time to catch sight of him as he dashed back into the entry to the catacombs. The two officers left their car running just feet from Dubois's limp body and sprinted into the entryway. Recapturing the escaped prisoner took priority in that frantic moment, but the chase ended immediately. Nostradamus had not bolted down the dark stairway as the police thought. He instead waited just inside the doorway and heaved both officers down the stairs into the blackness below.

Then he sprinted to their still-running electric Volkswagen Golf patrol car, stomped on the accelerator, and raced east on Boulevard Arago, to Boulevard Saint-Marel, then Boulevard de l'Hôpital, and the River Seine. He blew through two red lights, barely missed a man and his wife crossing the street at the first, and was nearly broadsided at the second. It didn't matter to the madman. He could taste and smell freedom, and he wanted more. So he raced onto the arched Pont d'Austerlitz bridge, crossed the low median, and ditched the car on the sidewalk, just inches from the low, concrete railing. As he sat atop the railing and threw his legs over it, he saw police cars converging from both ends of the bridge. Passersby walking close enough heard his diabolical laugh as he dropped over the side of the bridge onto an excursion boat packed with tourists just casting off below for what they thought would be a routine trip.

"Off! Now! Into the river! All of you!" Nostradamus shouted to the crowd on board.

But everyone froze in a terrified panic. So the crazed escapee grabbed the largest man near to him, lifted him high over his head, and threw him overboard. That broke the spell, and everyone abandoned the ship in a heartbeat. With no one to stop him, Nostradamus steered the boat away from the dock while the police watched helplessly from the bridge above. They drew their weapons but didn't fire them, fearing they might hit innocent civilians swimming frantically in all directions to escape from the maniac who had just hijacked their ride.

It took just minutes for Nostradamus to travel up the Seine to the Pont d'Iéna bridge near the Eiffel Tower, where he shut the engine off, donned the hoodie and jacket left on the boat by the pilot, jumped to the dock, and disappeared into the crush of midday tourists.

"You are doomed, Rafe!" Nostradamus declared in his head as he shouldered his way through the crowd in the shadow of the Iron Lady. "I don't know how. I don't know where or when. But someday soon, I will find you and make you pay for helping to lock me away like a common criminal! So wherever you are, prepare yourself for the wrath that is in store for you!"

Nostradamus, the madman, was loose in the world once again. Fortunately for Rafe and the President's Dozen, Gabriel Chastain, the hero legionnaire, was free once again as well.

8

PREPARING FOR THE DRAGON

A week later, alone on a deserted floor in a near-empty barracks on Orange-Caritat Air Base, a little more than 400 miles south of Paris, Rafe found four handsome, new pieces of luggage beside his bunk when he returned from breakfast. Each was meticulously packed. The smallest was filled with nicely folded pajamas, robes, and slippers, as well as a hefty, veau velours calfskin toiletry kit, complete with a straight razor, strop, Taylors of Old Bond Street almond shave cream, and a badger hair shaving brush. Two of the larger bags held various casual shirts, pants, shoes, underwear, and more.

The fourth piece, a bifold garment bag, provided Rafe with the clearest picture regarding the Jacques Saint-Pallet character he was to play on the trip. He unzipped the bag and found three expensive, casual, bespoke suits: a navy-blue Camps de Luca double-breasted pinstripe, a relaxed Artling two-button camel hair, and a beige Cifonelli linen wide lapel. Each was a hand-sewn work of art, beautifully tailored and wonderful to the touch. He carefully lifted each of them out of the bag and laid them side by side on his bunk. For a moment, he stood beside the bunk transfixed. He'd never dreamed he'd wear such fine clothes.

An awkward grin spread across his face when he recalled tossing rumpled jeans and t-shirts into a duffle for the trip. For more than two decades, he draped himself in either the legion's desert combat fatigues or a khaki officer's dress uniform. While lost in the civilian wilderness during the past eighteen months, he wore only t-shirts and jeans he bought in secondhand shops. Now there he was, outfitted to impress his fellow travelers as an obviously successful international travel writer. Rafe was fully convinced he would look the part. He was still standing there, letting it soak in, when Commandant Laurent came through the door looking for him.

"I hope you like them," Laurent said sincerely.

"What's not to like?" Rafe replied honestly.

"I wanted to have them ready for you well before the trip. So I sent what I hoped was a suitable stand-in to Paris to be measured. Try them on soon and let me know how they fit."

"I will," Rafe said as casually as he could manage so that he didn't sound too impressed. "But I think I'll shower and shave first. I'll want the full effect when I slip into them. I can see Monsieur Saint-Pallet is an even more successful writer than I had guessed. I only hope I can pull off the masquerade."

"I'm sure you'll be spectacular," Laurent replied. "You've always pulled off whatever France has asked of you. And you've always done it with a flare that distinguished your efforts."

"You don't have to say those things just because I kicked your ass, Laurent," Rafe said with a sarcastic, self-satisfied seriousness.

"Believe me, the ass-kicking has nothing to do with it," Laurent said flatly. "I may have even deserved it for having said things I shouldn't have about your heroic friend. But whatever the case, it could never erase your remarkable service career."

"Nope … but it sure as hell wiped it out," Rafe said with a clenched jaw.

"But not indelibly," Laurent reminded the former legionnaire. "I prefer to focus on this once-in-a-lifetime chance to watch our imperfect system right that wrong when you prove how mistaken they were about your honorable intentions."

"You're beginning to sound like you actually believe that," Rafe said cautiously.

"I do, so help me God," Laurent said as he stepped close enough to put a hand on Rafe's shoulder. "I was out of line to disparage Legionnaire Chastain's record the way

I did. I lost sight of his remarkable service to France just long enough to earn the lesson you taught me. I deeply regret that once you administered the lesson, the matter was out of my hands and you were caught up in a badly flawed system. No one asked me what I thought of the charges they filed against you. I'm deeply sorry it doesn't work that way—almost sorry enough to let you hit me one more time if I didn't know how much it would hurt. Still, I hope you can see your way to move past it by the time you set off on this mission. But whatever the case, I've already filed my support for the legion's recommendation that President DuPris expunge your record and reinstate you along with a promotion."

"Thank you, Laurent. I appreciate it," Rafe said and extended his hand for a shake.

"I consider it an honor, Legionnaire," Laurent replied and shook Rafe's hand firmly.

Rafe worked out with renewed discipline during the two weeks before he left for his ride on the *Dragon*. Each day began and ended with a five-mile run. Each afternoon included a two-hour swim. Frequent conversations with Laurent about the mission gave him a deeper understanding of what he might accomplish and a deeper appreciation of how the impression he made aboard the train could help him do it. His new clothes fit like a comfortable glove, and he wanted to look as though he knew and expected as much.

Unbeknownst to Rafe, while he worked out in the south

of France, the madman who called himself Nostradamus roamed the back streets of Paris, searching for him in anger and in vain. And neither of them knew that destiny would soon bring them together.

MEANWHILE, FAR AWAY IN NORTHERN MONTANA, RAFE'S sister, Madeleine, and her husband, Noah, prepared for the trip as well. They'd packed their bags early on and had settled into frequent rehearsals of being strangers on a train. Noah's role as Omar Keller, the Swizz custom and collector sword salesman, came to him naturally so he could focus on memorizing "the story" of his job and life he would share with passengers on the long trip. Madeleine, on the other hand, had difficulty warming up to the role of the flirtatious Italian socialite, Ariana Marie Russo, who supposedly had won a seat aboard the *Dragon* with a lucky lottery ticket.

"I must say, the light of the setting sun on your features and in your eyes makes you look particularly handsome this evening, Mr. Keller," Madeleine said to her husband as she approached him on the front porch of their home near Flathead Lake after supper. "Quite handsome indeed," she said tenderly as her hand gently brushed a lock of hair from his forehead.

"I would feel much more comfortable if you used my

real name when you say things like that to me," Noah said with a touch of irritation.

"I thought we were practicing," Madeleine replied defensively. "Noah? Are you getting jealous already? If you are, we probably shouldn't accept this mission. Tell me now and spare me the shopping I still need to do next week."

"Oh, I'll be okay with it, Madeleine," Noah reassured her. "It's just still so new to me. I've never experienced your flirting quite this way before."

"But I sincerely flirted with you when we were getting to know one another in Italy," the attractive brunette told her strapping husband. "Surely you can tell the difference between that and what you're hearing now. Frankly, I believe men are only comfortable with lighthearted flirting from women they hardly know. They may feel flattered, but they probably want nothing lasting to come of it, don't you think?"

"Hell, I don't know what sort of men you'll meet on that train, Madeleine," Noah said anxiously. "Neither you nor I know what they'll want or do. I'm just concerned for your safety."

"How many successful missions have we been on together?" she asked him with a smile. "Surely by now, you believe I can handle myself. Give this girl a little credit, would ya'?"

"You're right ... of course," Noah said softly with a knowing smile of his own. "Sorry."

"No need to feel sorry," she assured him. "Hold me in your arms and kiss me, my love."

About that time, atop Q's two calmest horses, Louis and Jenny were watching the sun slip behind Blacktail Mountain. Q and his wife, Marsha, took in the sight often with Doc and Connie. But it was new to the two Marines, who had only recently begun riding with the couples.

"How beautiful it is here!" Jenny sighed and sagged back into her saddle at the sight.

"We never get tired of it, that's for sure," Marsha told her. "Moving to Montana and Flathead Lake has been the best of the blessings to come from the risky work you all do."

"I seem to remember you're being involved in it now and then as well, young lady," Q piped up and reminded her.

"Only when circumstances demanded it, Q," she replied hastily.

"You're not going to try to tell me you didn't enjoy it at least a little, are you?" Q asked with a raised eyebrow.

"Maybe just a little, a time or two," Marsha sheepishly answered. "But, I'm ready to retire ... and you should be ready too, pretty soon, my dear."

"Happy wife, happy life!" Doc added to the conversation.

"Who would you fuss with if I retired, Doc?" Q asked only half-jokingly.

"He has a point, John," Connie joined in next. "Unless, of course, you retire too. You both can certainly afford to enjoy a life of leisure ... and heaven knows you have both earned it."

"Amen to that, sister," Marsha chuckled. "It would be wonderful to have help mucking out the stalls. We have a dozen horses now, Q, in case you've lost count. And they miss you when you're gone."

"Well, I'm glad to know someone does," Q replied with a chuckle of his own. "And mucking out stalls isn't my idea of a life of leisure."

"All this talk about horse manure has me thinking about the mess Noah and Madeleine and Tuck might be walking into when they step aboard that train in Shanghai," Doc said softly with a furrowed brow. "If they run into trouble before reaching Western Europe, we'll be unable to help them."

"That's China's doing, Doc," Louis said matter-of-factly. "They're running the show and calling the shots. Madeleine and the guys know we'd be on board with 'em if it were possible. They also know how to quickly size up situations and take care of themselves,"

"He's right, Doc," Jenny said with certainty. "It's all very true. The best we can do now is to prepare and be ready to improvise, adapt and overcome if the mission starts to go south."

"Spoken like a true Marine," Q told her with an approving grin. "I'd ride with you and this husband of yours anytime."

"Roger that!" Doc added with enthusiasm. "We should head back before it gets dark. Q goes to bed early these days, you know."

"That has nothing to do with my age and everything to do with the beautiful woman I married," Q said and flashed Marsha a devilish grin.

"I wish!" she sighed and wheeled her pinto pony, "Little Bean," around toward home.

The others enjoyed a laugh and fell in close behind.

The night was several hours old in Virginia. Tuck sat on the stoop in front of his Alexandria home, sipping a cup of hot valerian root tea. He hoped it would help him sleep. He hadn't slept much lately. He was getting less and less as his appointment with the *Dragon* grew nearer. With a loon calling somewhere in the night, Tuck wrestled with conflicting emotions. He was happy about being able to spend time with old friends soon. But he was sad that Eleanor wouldn't be with him. He was excited about experiencing a new engineering wonder of the world but apprehensive about what dangers might be waiting aboard it.

"I wish you were here, Eleanor," he whispered softly to the starry sky. "You'd know what to say to calm my heart and mind. Just the sound of your voice would do it. I miss you, honey."

Four hours later, the tea had had no effect, and Tuck was still awake. He had given up on the novel he'd tried to get interested in and found nothing worth watching after two trips through 150 cable channels. The digital clock beside his bed said *2:13 a.m.,* so it was 7:30 a.m. in London, and Tuck recalled that his friend Captain Michaels was an early riser. Tuck knew his cell phone's list of recent calls still contained the captain's number. He also knew his friend answered his own phone. So he propped himself against two pillows and punched the number.

"Top of the morning, Tuck!" Captain Michaels said cheerfully. "If you're in the States, why aren't you sleeping? If you're in London, why did you call instead of coming by?"

"No, I'm still in the States, Marty," Tuck chuckled. "I just couldn't sleep, and I thought, 'Hey, if I can't sleep, why should I let Marty rest?' So how's your trip preparation going?"

"Just swimmingly!" the captain said happily. "But to be honest, that's all done for us. We just have to pick out the clothes we wish to take, and it all gets bundled up for us. It did take some doing to make them understand that we don't wish to make any fashion statements on this trip, that we just want to be casual and comfortable. You know the look, I'm sure, old friend."

"It must be nice," Tuck sighed, looking at his still-empty luggage in a far corner of his bedroom. "How are you and the princess doing? Fine, I hope. I bet she's excited about the trip."

"Ahhh, she's as giddy as a schoolgirl, old chap!" the captain laughed. "She received quite a catalog of promotional material about the *Dragon*, and she's read it all twice already. The Chinese clearly intend to sell the Empire as many *Dragon*s as they can. So I'd appreciate your help in keeping her excitement under control on this journey, if you know what I mean."

"I'll do my best," Tuck laughed, "but from what I recall, that won't be easy. I won't keep you much longer, Marty. But I'd like to ask you how you're feeling about security on this trip. Are you at all apprehensive? Has MI6 talked with you about the precautions they're taking?"

"Oh yes, Tuck!" the captain stated confidently. "They're doing their homework, for sure. We'll be in good hands, as usual, I assure you. I can't share the details, you understand. But I assure you there's no need to worry about not bringing your own security. I've made it abundantly clear to them that the last thing England wants is to have to apologize to the Yanks for any embarrassing occurrences on this trip. You can rest easy about all that, my friend."

"Oh, I'm not worried at all, Marty, really," Tuck said almost apologetically.

"Well, you should be able to sleep well then," the captain said as he wound down the call. "I, on the other hand, have a busy morning ahead of me. I'll ring you up next week once our itinerary is finalized. But for now, goodnight and sweet dreams, my friend. Oh, please tell President Prescott the princess and I send our congratulations on his reelection."

"Thanks, Marty," Tuck replied. "I'll be sure to. Thanks for talking to me about all this."

"It was my pleasure, Tuck!" the captain said cheerfully. "Goodbye for now!"

Tuck felt better as he set his phone on the nightstand. Minutes later, he was sound asleep.

A LITTLE MORE THAN 400 MILES SOUTHEAST OF PARIS, Rafe was doing his best to focus on the positives of the mission ahead, the reunion with his sister, and the prospect of having his court-martial reversed. But, he struggled with many of the same concerns about the upcoming trip that kept Tuck awake at night. And it wasn't only the mission that troubled him.

The months since his ouster from the French Foreign Legion had been difficult. For the first time in his life, he had no cause, no home, and he felt like he had no country. The truth was that he was at the end of his rope when the legion's Gendarmerie Nationale found him and very likely saved his life.

Feeling good about himself for the first time in months, Rafe wondered how his only friend, Gabriel Chastain, was bearing up under the pressures of imprisonment and the pain of being ostracized by the legion he'd devoted his life to. Most of all, he worried his friend might not be getting the treatment he needed for the delusions that ravaged his mind and ruined his life.

Of course, Chastain *wasn't* getting the treatment he needed. If he had been, he likely would not have made his escape from Prison La Santé and be hiding out in a Saint-Denis slum on the northern outskirts of Paris. Even more tragically, he might not still be suffering under the delusion that he was the legendary seer, Nostradamus. The few people he interacted with in the hours following his escape laughed at him and kept walking. When his hopes of finding a benefactor to buy him a meal were thwarted and night closed in, he broke into the rear of a shuttered market and made off with a day-old baguette and a large wedge of mimolette cheese.

As Nostradamus headed deep into another alley with his supper, a thunderstorm approached from the north, and rain began to fall. So he huddled among some trash cans beneath a tattered awning. He found an empty jar in one of the trash cans and set it beyond the awning to catch the rainwater he used to wash down the bread and cheese. While he waited for the rain to slow enough for him to search for a safe, dry place to sleep, his mind slipped deeper into delusion, and his anger grew.

The world would laugh and scoff to see you in this circumstance, Nostradamus, a voice inside his mind told him. *You are wise, but they do not listen to you. You are mighty, but they want only to lock you away with no regard for your warnings of the dangers to come. Now you are free once again. And you will spend every waking moment searching for the man who helped lock you up. You will exact your revenge. He will live just long enough to regret ever crossing your path, and he will pay the ultimate price for his treachery.*

As the rain slowed, Nostradamus stepped out from under the awning and began his search for a secure hiding place where he could finally get some rest on the first night of his newfound freedom. He headed back in the direction of the market he broke into earlier two alleys away. His plan was to shelter there if he didn't find a better alternative on the way. The darkness of that moonless night provided his cover along the dimly lit streets and alleys. He hadn't seen police or a patrol car since he eluded them that afternoon. He hoped to keep it that way. But just a few yards out of the ally, he heard what sounded to him like a woman's muffled scream. In the darkness, he caught a glimpse of a woman being dragged around a corner into an ally up ahead.

He silently sprinted to the ally, rounded the corner, and saw a tall, heavyset man in a worn-out trench coat ripping the woman's jacket from her body with one of his large, grimy hands while he covered her mouth with the other. She couldn't breathe, and her slight body went limp as Nostradamus drew near and sprang at the brute who had snatched her.

"Pick on someone your own size!" the seer sneered as he grabbed his target by the shoulders from behind and shook the creep so hard he let go of his victim.

"Let's do it!" the clueless brute growled and took a vicious swing at Nostradamus.

"Let's not!" Nostradamus growled back as he dodged the man's punch. "You're no match for me, you animal!"

In a single, smooth arc, the ex-legionnaire dodged another punch, snatched an empty metal trash can by one of its handles, and smashed into the brute's skull with a loud, crunching thud. The witless target crumpled to the ground in a heap as the seer moved in close and raised the trash can for another go at cracking his victim's skull wide open.

"Stop!" the terrified woman shouted. "He's had enough! Don't kill him!"

"He deserves to die," Nostradamus told her matter-of-factly.

"We all do, and we will, one day," she replied. "But that must be God's doing, not ours."

"God's a luxury I've never had in my life," Nostradamus told her cynically.

"The man's unconscious," she told her hero. "I'll call the police and have him arrested. I'm grateful for your fast action. You may have saved my life, and I am most thankful!"

"It was my pleasure, Ms ... Ugh, I don't even know your name," the hero admitted.

"I'm Genevieve Valoir," she said. "And you are?"

"Nostradamus, milady," he told her with a slight bow.

"No, really," she chuckled. "What's your name? I should at least know the name of the man I will tell my friends and family about ... not to mention the police, whenever they arrive."

"My full name is Michel de Nostredame," he said softly. "But I'm known simply as Nostradamus around the world."

"But Nostradamus was born early in the sixteenth century, and you don't look a day over thirty-five," she said with a smile to humor him. "How do you explain that?"

"I can't," he told her flatly. "But there are *many* things I can't explain. How about you?"

"On that, I must agree," she conceded. "And I need to call the police, or I will have to explain what took me so long to do so."

"Must you call them?" Nostradamus asked sheepishly. "I have to leave if you do."

"But why?" she asked urgently. "Are you a criminal too?"

"In the eyes of the world, I am," he sighed. "But not in my heart and mind."

"I suppose that man on the ground might give me the same answer," she said.

"But I'm telling the truth … and *he's* likely a liar as well as a mugger," he answered. "What are you doing out on the streets alone at this hour, anyway?"

"This is my way to and from work each day," she said. "I've never had trouble before."

"Well, tonight, you got more trouble than I suspect you ever imagined," he said.

"You are right about that," she replied. "But I really must call the police now."

Nostradamus was captivated by her beauty when he got his first good look at her face in the light from her cell phone. He hated to leave, but he knew he must. So he silently vanished into the darkness of the alley while she focused on the call and answered the officer's questions.

"They'll be here any minute …" she started to explain but gasped when she realized her hero had vanished as suddenly as he had appeared.

By the time the police arrived and loaded Genevieve's assailant into the back of their patrol car, Nostradamus was getting comfortable in the back room of the market he'd broken into earlier. He was exhausted and fell asleep almost immediately. But it was a fitful sleep. He dreamed Rafe was on a journey far away, aboard a huge, bizarre-looking train that flew at an amazing speed less than an inch above the ground. In the dream, Rafe traveled many miles with many people from many countries ... and they were all bound for Paris. But the train suddenly exploded and was engulfed in a huge fireball that was so real it jolted Nostradamus awake in a terrifying cold sweat.

That treacherous bastard must not die in an explosion! the voice in the seer's mind told him. *You must be waiting for him when he reaches Paris and kill him with your own two hands! You've earned the right after the suffering he's caused you ... and he deserves such a fate because he was the cause of your suffering!*

Nostradamus was now a man with a mission, macabre though it was. He snuck out the back door of the market before the morning shift arrived and walked the streets determined to make sense of the dream. He knew it held the key to the revenge he thirsted for. And he swore he would find the key and be ready and waiting when Rafe arrived in Paris.

ON THE EVE OF THE *DRAGON*'S DEPARTURE, THE TIME FOR wondering, worrying, guessing, hoping, dreaming, and preparing had come to a glorious, exciting end. Madeleine arrived in Shanghai two days prior. Noah got there just eighteen hours in advance, barely time to get a room, shower, and change clothes. Rafe's plane touched down at Shanghai Pudong International Airport near midnight, just nine hours before he would see his compartment onboard the train. He was fine with the short time he had. He'd slept well on the flight from Nice; so well, in fact, that he'd slept right through the forty-minute refueling and crew-change stopover in Baghdad.

Tuck, however, spent the entire prior week traveling casually with his friends, Captain Michaels and Princess Mary, making several stops along the way to Shanghai. They finally arrived in time for supper the night before the start of the *Dragon*'s epic voyage. He was astonished by the crush of press and electronic media that swarmed the airport and along the highway from the airport to their hotel.

"Is it like this everywhere the two of you travel?" he asked the royal couple.

"Not really, old boy," the captain chuckled. "I'm afraid Mary and I have become very old news in the rest of the world."

"Actually, I suspect their coverage here in China will be more about their marvelous *Dragon* than about us," Mary said. "I'm quite sure the media thinks our visit says more about the superiority of Chinese engineering and technology than it does about our interest in the future."

"You can hardly get more capitalistic than that," Tuck said with a smile.

Meanwhile, Doc, Q, Jenny, and Louis were huddled on two park benches they'd set face-to-face overlooking St. James Park Lake near the heart of London. They had a far easier schedule than the other team members had in Shanghai. While the four aboard the *Dragon* would spring into action in just a few hours, Doc and those he kiddingly called his "Western Europe Contingent" had another week to get into place and prepare for whatever action the *Dragon* might bring their way.

"What are we in for, Doc? Really?" Q asked his leader and friend.

"I've told you all I know, Q, ... which is as much as you already know," Doc sighed. "What you and I both also know is that the president only tells us as much as he can. Sometimes, it's all he knows. Other times, it's all he's able to divulge without jeopardizing national security. And there's no way we can know the difference in advance. Other times, we may never know, not even years later. We both know that better than we're comfortable with. That's why we just focus on the mission and leave the rest to history."

"Yeah, well, spending a week and a half in Paris on the government's dime hardly seems like a mission," Q told him. "It sure as hell is unlike any we've ever been on."

"Are you complaining, Q?" Doc asked incredulously. "You're on the best assignment of your life, and you're uncomfortable with it? What's wrong with this picture?"

"Nothing comes for free … especially in this business," Q said in near-frustration. "I just want to make sure we don't relax so much that we can't respond effectively if this thing blows up."

"Then focus," Doc said simply. "But don't get wound so tight that you respond badly. It's business as usual, Q. Do what you do best. Focus on the positives, be ready for anything and enjoy the ride. If you can't do that in Paris, you're definitely ready for retirement."

"There's that word again," Q chuckled. "A bet's a bet. You owe me a hundred bucks!"

"You tricked me!" Doc said with a suspicious laugh.

"Like you said about this mission, old friend. You may never know for sure," Q told him with a broad grin, and Jenny and Louis got a good look at the unique bond Doc and Q enjoyed.

"It's time to focus, everyone," Doc said with renewed seriousness. "You'll each be on a plane early tomorrow. You've got your instructions. Once you're settled in at your destinations, hunker down, get familiar with the sights and routines at the train station the *Dragon* will travel through, and keep an eye out for suspicious activity," Doc reminded the team. "Any questions?"

"Can we expense souvenirs?" Jenny asked with a sly smile.

"You are *definitely* a member of this team," Doc said with a grin and a sigh. "But you spend too much time around

Q. If there are no serious questions, it's time to eat. I'm buying."

"Hallelujah!" Louis finally piped up. "This is my idea of a mission … at least so far."

"Do you think we can get a good bar burger here, Doc?" Q asked in his inimitable way.

9

THE ADVENTURE BEGINS

Rafe was the first member of the team to reach the Shanghai Railway Station the fateful morning. The handsome, square-jawed Frenchman cut a striking image as he strode toward the security phalanx in the near-empty north concourse. His muscular, 6'5" frame was impossible to miss wrapped in his perfectly tailored navy-blue double-breasted pinstripe suit.

He looked every bit the part of Jacques Saint-Pallet, a highly successful, globe-trotting travel writer. But the ex-legionnaire felt awkward being trailed by the elderly porter pushing a cart loaded with his luggage. Still, it felt good to tip the distinguished-looking porter with a 50-euro bill to ensure the bags got through security and onto the train. While the porter made that happen, Rafe made his way through the battery of security scans and passport checks before finally taking the first of three escalators for his rendezvous with the *Dragon*.

The hush of the near-empty concourse made the moment all the more surreal. The importance and seriousness of the voyage that was about to begin were palpable as he eyed the solemn-faced soldiers with automatic weapons who flanked his path, and he heard the low crackle of instructions and check-ins coming over the radios each of them wore. Then suddenly, as he descended the last escalator into the restricted section of the station, he got his first look at the *Dragon*. The sleek, missile-like, brand spanking new wonder of the world glistened in the lights that bathed it beside the platform, and it momentarily took his breath away. Neither he nor anyone else in the western hemisphere had ever seen anything quite like it ... especially in a railway station.

He felt only a little foolish backstepping on the escalator to give himself a few extra moments at what he was sure was the ideal vantage point to take in the monster machine most of the world didn't yet even know existed. Rafe was glad the escalator was empty because, for the first time in a very long time, he felt and acted like a schoolboy. Even better, he felt like a schoolboy on the verge of a major adventure. That excited him in a way he needed. It invigorated him beyond anything he'd experienced while reading about or talking about the *Dragon*. Now here it was, and the battle-hardened tough guy felt butterflies in his stomach and smiled as he stepped aboard car number eight.

"Bonjour, Monsieur Saint-Pallet!" the pretty Mei Yin

said to him in near-perfect French. "Welcome aboard the *Dragon!*"

The Frenchman quickly noted the name on her name tag and very much enjoyed the view as the pretty young woman led the way to his private compartment.

"Merci Beaucoup, Mei Yin!" he told her sincerely at the door of his compartment, and he hoped he'd see her again soon.

Noah was the next to arrive. He hoped his nervousness wasn't showing as he handed his "new" passport and ID to the security officer at the station's first checkpoint.

"Welcome, Mr. Keller," the officer said to him as he handed back the documents. "You're very fortunate to be included on this adventure."

"I am indeed!" Noah replied with relief and quickly progressed through the body scanners, then practically ran to the bank of escalators.

Noah's first look at the *Dragon* had much the same effect on him as it did on Rafe. But the attendant on car number seven did not. His was an older, stodgy gentleman who was clearly just going through the motions. He hardly spoke during the walk to Noah's compartment and gave only yes or no answers to his questions. It wasn't at all the welcome Noah had anticipated. As he plopped down on the armchair beside what looked like a very comfortable bed, he chuckled at the thought of how Madeleine likely would have handled the old guy.

Madeleine purposely arrived just twenty-eight minutes before the *Dragon* was scheduled to leave the station. Unlike the others, her role was to attract as much attention as possible. And she was determined to live out the role of the well-dressed, very coquettish Ariana Marie Russo. Her arrival at the north entrance of the station was a chaotic whirlwind of a comic, almost-breathless rush to not miss the train. She burst through the glass automatic double doors wearing a clinging, red, floor-length, sequined gown, topped by a bright pink feather boa and a broad-brimmed, rose-colored hat that had a three-inch crimson band. A small cadre of young and old male porters trailed behind her, each carrying at least two of her bags.

"You really must hurry!" she told everyone she interacted with in any airport or security capacity. "I simply cannot be kept from getting to my train on time!"

The sequins on her gown kept setting off the security alarm at the scanners. A female security officer used a wand on her, but the alarm went off even louder.

"You really should have better machines!" she huffed and stamped a foot. "I will not let you make me miss my train."

"I'm very sorry, miss. But I cannot let you through until you are cleared by the scanners," the attendant told her dutifully.

"It's okay, Sophia," a very distinguished-looking older

gentlemen interjected softly. "I personally vouch for Ms. Russo and will escort her to the *Dragon*."

The well-dressed gentleman gave Madeleine a warm smile and offered her his arm.

"It's an honor to meet you, Ms. Russo," he said. "I'm Mr. Li, director of the station. Please allow me to show you the way."

"Why, what a gentleman you are!" Madeleine gushed to Mr. Li. "And handsome too!"

Mr. Li blushed and stuttered all the way to the bottom of the last escalator.

"Oh my goodness!" Madeleine exclaimed when she saw the *Dragon*. "Is that it?"

"That's it," Mr. Li said with a boyish grin. "Do you like it?"

"Why, it's so big!" Madeleine said to him with deliberate breathlessness. "I don't know if I can take it all in at once!"

The look on Mr. Li's face when he heard her blatant double-entendre was exactly what Madeleine had hoped for. It encouraged her in the role she was secretly beginning to enjoy. He accompanied her all the way to her compartment aboard car number nine, stayed until the very last minute, and handed her his business card as the signal sounded to warn that the *Dragon* was about to leave the station.

"If ever I can be of any help to you in any way, Ms. Russo, don't hesitate to call me," he said with an impish grin.

"Oh, I certainly will," Madeleine said with a smile as she tucked the card into the bodice of her gown. "Thank you for your kind assistance, Mr. Li. Arrivederci!" she said as he left.

Tuck had already been aboard the *Dragon* for nearly two hours before Rafe arrived at the station. He, the captain, and the princess had arrived in Shanghai four days in advance of "Embarkment Day" and were immediately swept up in China's interpretation of "the royal treatment." A gleaming, gold-colored, Chinese-manufactured Hongqi N501 was waiting for them on the tarmac when they landed at Shanghai Pudong International Airport. The princess was presented with an armful of red roses before being escorted to the limo, which ferried her and the two retired naval captains to the Grand Hyatt hotel in the heart of downtown Shanghai.

Dozens of more flowers and three enormous fruit baskets graced both of the adjoining four-bedroom, five-bath penthouse suites they enjoyed the use of while they relaxed and prepared for their trip aboard the *Dragon*. While waiting for their luggage to be delivered, Tuck and Captain Michaels stood at floor-to-ceiling windows in the living room and took in the dramatic view of the Shanghai skyline and the Huangpu River, thirty-five stories below them, winding its way to the Yellow Sea.

"What an absolutely breathtaking view!" Princess Mary said as she joined them and put an arm around her husband's waist. "This city is so alive with people, sights, and sounds that it makes me want to spend a couple of weeks here exploring every inch of it. It's wonderful to be here," she said with a sigh. "And it's wonderful that you could join us, Tuck. I'm so glad we have this time to reconnect. It's been far too long since last we saw you. Life does get away from us, doesn't it?"

"It most certainly does, ma'am ... ugh, Mary." Tuck awkwardly fumbled with the convention the princess hated most about being the daughter of the Queen of England. She had already reminded him once that he should simply call her Mary, as she asked of most everyone who spent time around her. She never made a fuss about the formal address accorded to her upon a first meeting, but she refused to otherwise ever be called Your Royal Highness, or even the more-ordinary royal moniker, "ma'am."

"You both look so very handsome," she said with a smile. "We really must have some pictures taken before you get comfortable. I promised Mum we'd have lots of them taken and send them at least once every day so she can follow our progress. She's still such a mother. It makes me laugh and sometimes cry."

The hotel promptly sent a photographer to their suites and promised to have prints delivered within the hour.

When the photo session was over, Tuck changed out of his suit and into an outfit Madeleine had found and bought for him on one of her several pre-mission shopping excursions. He'd tried to tell her he had more than enough clothes for the trip, but she insisted on buying the ensemble and shipping it to him in Alexandria the week before he left to join the captain and the princess in England.

"Oh, let me have some fun shopping for someone who will spend time with the princess," she insisted. "It's on the president's dime," she said. "He insisted that I put all my trip-related purchases on his personal charge card. He'll understand. He better!"

Tuck could tell from the sound of her voice that it would do no good to argue, so he conceded and hoped for the best. He was quite pleasantly surprised when the package arrived just days later, and he unwrapped a very chic, pale gray, linen Cubavera shirt and pants set. It fit perfectly and felt comfortable when he first tried them on. And he was pleased to wear them to dinner with his friends in their suite.

The rest of the trio's time in the city was spent on well-planned, chauffeured sightseeing drives in a short convoy of armored vehicles, accompanied by a phalanx of motorcycles and flashing lights for added security.

"It's impossible for you two to be inconspicuous, I see," Tuck chuckled in his rear-facing seat during the first such outing.

"They mean well," the princess said with a gracious smile. "I can't imagine how much preparation the Chinese government must have invested in our visit. And the planning that must have gone into our trip aboard the *Dragon* is beyond comprehension."

"I'm quite certain they feel the potential dividends far outweigh their investment, my dear," the captain told his wife.

"Roger that!" Tuck replied.

"Roger who?" the princess innocently asked.

"It's just an American military expression, my dear," the captain told her.

The princess and the captains were already settled in and had begun exploring the *Dragon* by the time Rafe, Madeleine, and Noah were aboard. As the first signal was sounded that the *Dragon* would soon begin its voyage, the royal party took seats on the observation deck above the forward-most dining car. They occupied the first row on the left, while the four British Special Air Service officers assigned to protect the princess, the captain and Tuck surrounded them: two in the seats immediately behind them, the other two in the front row to the royal party's right.

"Will we be this closely guarded by the SAS the entire trip?" Tuck asked nervously.

"Not at all, old boy," the captain chuckled. "Just when we're in settings that make them anxious. They originally tried to convince us to avoid the observation decks for fear we would be too visible and exposed to sniper fire. But I convinced them that there aren't enough snipers in the entire world for there to be one at precisely the right place, at precisely the right time."

"Was it a hard sell?" Tuck asked, only half kiddingly.

"Not nearly as hard as some," the captain chuckled. "Actually, I suspect they really saw it as an opportunity to enjoy the view as well."

When the second signal sounded, excitement noticeably grew among the passengers. They knew it meant the *Dragon* would awaken in exactly five minutes. Tuck sat back in the comfortable high-back leather chair and focused on the sensory input of the experience. He noted that the ambient lighting began to slowly dim, and he guessed it was designed to lend power to the natural light he knew would flood through the windowed walls and ceiling of the observation deck the moment the *Dragon* emerged from the depths of the station into the open air of Shanghai. The soft, low, classical music that had wafted through the train since he and the royals boarded began to fade out, and Tuck guessed it would soon be replaced by upbeat tunes to cheer everyone on board when the *Dragon* began to roll.

As the digital clock/speedometer at the top-center of the front wall of the car counted down, Tuck was surprised and a bit concerned to see attendants enter the car carrying drinks on trays just moments before the lurch he anticipated would jostle them when the train began to roll. But he was momentarily distracted by the surprise of suddenly hearing the Beatles' classic hit "Here Comes the Sun" with just five seconds left on the countdown clock. Then he turned his attention back to the clock, clenched his jaw, and prepared to stifle a laugh when the lurch of the train's takeoff came, and the drinks on the attendants' trays launched onto unfortunate passengers. He felt his breath quicken as he counted down quietly, "Five, four, three, two, one."

But to Tuck's great surprise, there was no lurch, no jolt when the *Dragon* came alive. Instead, the sensation was much like being ever-so-gently turned in a sturdy swivel chair. The attendants comfortably continued serving drinks without so much as a ripple, let alone a splash.

Imagine that, he thought while "Here Comes the Sun" resounded throughout the observation deck, and the *Dragon* emerged from the depths of the station into the bright sunlight of that Shanghai morning.

"Well, it looks and sounds like the Chinese have thought of every detail for this trip," Tuck said to his friends beside him.

"This is about as 'British' as anyone could get," Captain Michaels quipped.

While Tuck pondered just how much of a marvel the *Dragon* might prove to be on the trip, he set his feet upon the footrest in front of him and fixed his eyes upon the speedometer at the top-center of the wall in front of him. Though he felt only the slightest movement, the speedometer told quite a different story. A half-mile from the platform—where the rear half of the *Dragon* was still rolling—its speedometer seemed to go wild. In the blink of an eye, it climbed to *KPH: 80,* then *KPH: 100 ... 150 ... 180* less than a minute from the station. Acceleration continued as a pretty, young attendant paused at Tuck's aisle seat and flashed him a professional smile.

"Would any of you like to toast this momentous adventure?" she asked and presented a tray of six rock-steady glasses of champagne.

The princess declined, but the captains each readily accepted a glass and took a couple of sips before setting their glasses on tray tables that unfolded from within the arms of their seats.

Amazing, Tuck thought as he looked closely at the placid surface of the champagne in his glass, then glanced at the speedometer on the wall, which now read KPH: *270.7.*

We're moving at more than 165 miles per hour, and it's as though we're standing still, he marveled silently. *If this machine can maintain anything even approaching this stability at 400 miles per hour, it's a modern-day engineering miracle!*

"Excuse me, miss," Tuck said softly to the attendant. "My name is Augustus Baird," he told her as he read her name tag. "May I call you Mei Yin?"

"Why yes, of course," she said cheerfully. "I would like that."

"Then please call me Tuck," he replied with a warm smile. "All my friends do."

"Tuck," she said thoughtfully. "It means neat and orderly. It suits you well."

"And what does Mei Yin mean?" Tuck asked her.

"Beauty," she said simply. "But of course, that is always in the eye of the beholder."

"I very much agree," he replied and left it to her to ponder whether he agreed that she was beautiful or that it depended on the beholder.

Meanwhile, Noah made his way to the concession counter located in the middle dining car. He was delighted to find complimentary coffee and absolutely thrilled to discover it offered a Swiss creamed expresso. He opted for a large cup and chose two small wedges of lemon sponge cake, then chose a corner table at a window. His first joyful sips of the hot brew helped him quickly unwind from the rigors of rising early, making his way to the station and running the security gauntlet to board the *Dragon* on time.

His seat afforded him a perfect place to people-watch while he savored his snack. The car bustled with passengers visibly excited to be aboard the *Dragon* and enjoying its amenities. His seat was comfortable and so close to the coffee bar he could smell each selection being poured. Freshly brewed coffee was definitely one of his weaknesses, and he happily took in the welcome waves of aromas.

Totally relaxed now, Noah took the liberty of putting his feet on the chair opposite his and settled back to enjoy the moment and the ride. The warmth of the sunlight coming through the large window relaxed him even more, and he began to feel as though he could nap right there at the table despite having already downed half of his expresso. But rather than close his eyes, he surveyed the growing crowd of passengers lined up for a morning beverage and a look at the freshly baked pastries. Noah was fascinated by the crush of people from so many different countries and cultures, speaking different languages. He was impressed by the Chinese government's wildly successful use of the *Dragon* to assemble such a diverse group from across two continents and introduce them to China's emergence as a twenty-first-century world power.

In the middle of that thought, Noah noticed a young male attendant who appeared out of sorts and out of place. Unlike the dozen or so other attendants Noah had seen that morning, this one wasn't smiling. He seemed to almost sneer at the crowd before him. The young man's angry demeanor was in odd contrast to the mood that pervaded the train. But Noah quickly wrote off the sight of one unhappy attendant as the product of an unknowable number of possible causes. Yet, the sight was in such contrast to everything else in the dining car that morning it made Noah sad to see it. So he noted the man's name tag said *Li Wei*, and he made a mental note to say something positive to the young man sometime later that day. Then he shifted his attention out the window for the first time. He was surprised at how fast and quietly the rural scenery raced by. The speedometer above the dining car's double doors read *KPH: 510*, and Noah wrestled with the reality that the *Dragon* was moving at more than 300 miles per hour and was still steadily gaining speed. His heart raced a bit in that moment as well, and he predictably began to wonder where Madeleine was and what she was up to.

He didn't have to wonder for long because she was headed his way. The time of day was the last thing on Madeleine's mind. When she first came aboard, she took a good amount of time to familiarize herself with her compartment. She thought her queen-size bed felt perfect and was more than pleased with the size of the bathroom and its comfy-looking soaking tub. She spent the next hour or so freshening up and slipped into her first change of clothes for the day. Then she applied a few touches of Chanel No. 5, chose a pair of comfortable shoes, and headed for the dining cars. Both aisles of the first one she entered were jammed with passengers excitedly greeting one another and marveling at the sights and sounds surrounding them. The tables were all occupied. So she moved on, into the first galley car, with its single aisle down the middle between two enclosed kitchens that hummed with busy staff preparing the day's lunch selections.

As Madeleine neared the door to the second dining car,

she nearly collided with a young male attendant who rushed by her without a word. The brash encounter startled her, and she was shocked by his seeming indifference to having almost knocked her down as he rushed by.

What the ... she thought, but refrained from asking. *He's no doubt had better days*! she thought as she stepped into the center dining car.

Noah saw her immediately and had to catch himself as he instinctively almost waved to her. He did make eye contact with his attractive, ornately dressed wife, and she flashed him a fleeting but endearing smile before she demurely stepped up to a table full of older gentlemen with another standing in the aisle speaking to them in English.

"Good morning," she said sweetly. "Do any of you gentleman happen to have the time?"

"For you, madam, I have all the time in the world," one of them said with a sly smile.

"It's almost 11 o'clock, ma'am," the gentleman standing said more innocently. "Get up and give the young lady a seat, fellas!" he barked.

"Oh, I'm just passing through," she told him softly. "But thank you for your kindness. Perhaps we'll have an opportunity to talk soon."

"I certainly hope so, madam. Have a wonderful day," the

gentleman replied while his friends just stared with their mouths open.

"And you as well!" she said, and her ruby red lips formed her best-practiced smile just before she moved on in the direction of the coffee bar.

Noah knew by the reactions of many of the men in the car it was safe to stare and smile at Madeleine as she moved through the crowd. He thought she looked fabulous, and he had a good laugh deep inside about the wardrobe bills President Prescott must have received by the time she had finished shopping for the trip.

Well, she warned him, Noah thought as he watched her. *And judging by the reactions of most of the men I can see, the president needn't worry whether he got his money's worth.*

Madeleine was caught off guard when the distinguished-looking older gentleman just ahead of her in the tea line offered her the last piece of bundt cake left beside the coffee urns.

"I think this last portion is meant for you, my dear," he told her in English with a thick accent she thought could be East Indian.

"Why, thank you," she replied softly and flashed him a genuine smile for his kindness.

Madeleine gladly accepted the offer and set the bundt cake on a small paper plate.

"Which tea are you having this morning?" she asked him with interest.

"Oh, I'm thrilled to have Masala Chai Tea with milk this morning," he said with a smile.

"That sounds perfect," she told him, though she'd never had it before. "Allow me to pour for both of us," she said and filled two large coffee cups.

"Please allow me to carry yours to your table," the gentleman offered.

"Oh, I don't have a table yet," she replied. "And I'm not at all sure one is available."

"Well, let's have a look," he said and led the way up the nearer of the two aisles.

Madeleine was thrilled when it began to look as though their search was going to take them by Noah's table. As they approached it, Noah took the cue and stood up.

"The two of you are welcome to share my table," he said with a smile.

"Why, how very kind of you, sir!" his wife gushed as a stranger might.

"Yes, you are so generous to welcome company on such a crowded morning," the older gentleman told Noah.

"My name is Omar Keller, and I'm very pleased to meet you both," Noah told them.

"How do you do," the gentleman replied. "My name is Choda Bhandari."

"And I'm Ariana Russo," Madeleine quickly added. "Ariana *Marie* Russo, that is."

"I'm so pleased that you both agreed to join me," Noah told them. "I really enjoy meeting new people, and this is such a grand opportunity to do that."

While the three of them enjoyed small talk about their hometowns, families, occupations, and how they happened to be on the *Dragon*, Rafe was headed their way. He could smell the coffee when he approached the transit link to the forward-most dining car. He paused just outside the door because he could see that two attendants (Mei Yin and Li Wei) were having an emotional conversation inside the transit link. He recognized Mei Yin when she raised her head.

"I know why we are here. Do you?" Li Wei angrily asked her.

"There is no harm in being friendly," Mei Yin timidly replied. "Why must you be so angry all the time?"

"These fools are not our friends!" Li Wei growled at her. "Why must I remind you?"

Rafe instinctively burst through the door and intervened when Li Wei raised a hand as if he was about to slap the young woman.

"Stop!" Rafe said firmly and snatched the young man's

wrist in mid-swing. "That's no way to treat a lady. Didn't you learn that growing up … or haven't you grown up yet?"

"This is none of your business!" Li Wei barked back at Rafe and quickly exited the transit.

"Are you okay, Mei Yin?" the former legionnaire asked gently.

"I am fine, really, Monsieur Saint-Pallet," she awkwardly assured him. "Thank you for your help. I must get back to work," she meekly added as she led the way into the dining car.

Noah spotted the two of them over Madeleine's shoulder and again caught himself before reflexively waving to the Frenchman. Madeleine knew by the look in his eyes and his body language that someone he knew had come into view behind her. But she didn't let on.

"I'm happy to see you again, so soon, Mei Yin," Rafe said softly. "But I'm sorry it's under such unfortunate circumstances. Uh … Mei Yin means beauty, doesn't it?"

The pretty young woman modestly nodded, "Yes,"

"Your parents named you perfectly," he said sincerely and held her glance for a moment. "I look forward to seeing you again soon. In the meantime, don't hesitate to find me if you have any more trouble with your co-worker."

"Thank you, but I'm certain that I won't," she quietly

answered as she turned to leave. "Thank you again for your assistance, Monsieur Saint-Pallet."

Rafe purposely avoided looking in Noah's direction and headed for the coffee bar. As he poured a cup of black coffee, he thought about the exchange he had interrupted, and he wondered what it was really about. He hoped it wasn't a lovers' quarrel. That would mean his efforts to get to know Mei Yin better would be all the more challenging. There was a lot Rafe didn't know about the incident he'd stumbled upon and the connection between Mei Yin and Li Wei. That detail would elude him for a few more days.

10

J ust off the coast of Newfoundland and 38,000 feet in the air, Doc, Jenny, Louis, and Q were huddled aboard President Prescott's personal 757, engaged in their familiar exercise of bouncing thoughts off one another about the mission.

"If you wanted to take the *Dragon*, how would you do it?" Doc asked the group.

"It seems to me that the only sure way to take something moving at more than 400 miles an hour would be to have people in place onboard," Louis answered thoughtfully.

"I'm thinking the same thing," Doc agreed. "Attempting an assault from the outside would be too big a gamble. There's too much potential for people and events onboard to scuttle an attack planned for a particular location and time, not to mention the complexity of having to breach the train once you've stopped it and then overpower the security forces onboard."

"But having people in place would also be a tricky proposition, wouldn't you say?" Jenny asked. "You gotta believe the Chinese took good, hard looks at the staff they have on board. Unless, of course, you're thinkin' the Chinese government could be behind such an attack."

"Or their military," Q added. "They might see this as an opportunity to spark conflicts they could exploit to China's advantage."

"What are you saying exactly, Q?" Doc prodded his friend.

"No one's been able to say for certain that the Chinese military isn't behind the Red Z bombings," Q explained. "Remember, zuìzhōng de zhēngfú means the *'ultimate conquest.'* That's not a very smart rallying cry for one small terrorist cell unless they have the backing of the military, which, in China, would only be possible if they also have the government's blessing."

"That's a pretty dark view of the Reds, Q," Doc replied. "But we can't rule it out, and that adds a lot more layers to this onion."

"So what you're saying is there's no telling how much resistance, if any, there will be onboard if an attack takes place," Louis concluded.

"I'm afraid you're right, at the moment, Louis," Doc

agreed. "And we may never know. So we must simply stay focused. Our mission is to help repel an attack, if it occurs, and at the very least extract the royals and our team members safely at any cost. Understood?"

"I understand, alright!" Q barked back. "We can't trust the Reds as far as we can throw 'em! I've understood that for years, Doc, and so have you. If I was onboard and anything funny happened, I'd have the whole crew against the wall with their hands over their heads. That's the only approach that'll ensure our people get off that damned train alive."

"You could be right, Q," Doc said. "Let's just hope we're overreacting to the few facts we have and that the trip ends without a hitch. I'll be thrilled if we find out when this mission is over that we were simply overreacting to the little we know and overthinking what it means."

"Still, the Red Z won't ever have another target like the *Dragon*," Louis countered. "China has wittingly or unwittingly created a perfect target, moving at more than 600 kilometers per hour across two continents. The brochure the passengers received before the trip called it the 'Voyage of a Lifetime!' But I can't shake the image of the *Titanic* striking that iceberg."

"It's actually quite ironic that you say that, Louis, because as we speak, we're close to the spot where it went down," Doc told him.

"No kidding?!" Louis gasped.

"No kidding," Doc said. "She sank about 325 nautical miles off the tip of Newfoundland."

"You can bet an assault on the *Dragon* would rank right alongside that tragedy," Q said ominously and added, "If they make a movie about it, I want Harrison Ford to play me."

AS DOC AND THE OTHERS LAUGHED, HIS SATELLITE PHONE vibrated. It was the president.

"Yes sir, Mr. President," Doc said, still laughing.

"Hello, Doc!" the president boomed over the line. "It's nice to hear someone happy to get my call for a change."

"I just heard Q and Harrison Ford mentioned in the same sentence," Doc chuckled.

"And I look forward to hearing you explain when we're face-to-face," the president said. "Right now, I've got some reading material for you and the team. The Situation Room is transmitting it, and you should have it momentarily. It's not an urgent matter," he said. "It's background intel about our friends, the Chinese."

"I'll read it as soon as it arrives," Doc assured him.

"It's material from this morning's briefing. It won't take long to read," the president told him. "Call me back when you've read it."

"Roger that, Mr. President," Doc replied as the president ended the call.

"A change of plan?" Jenny asked as Doc put his phone away.

"No, but my gut tells me the current one might have just gotten muddied-up," Doc sighed and headed for the plane's office space. "I'll be right back," he told the team.

Doc entered the office and stood beside what he called the President's FAX machine. It was far more complicated than that. But it did pretty much the same thing … just more securely. Seconds later, the machine spit out three blank sheets of paper. Doc then entered a ten-digit code into the lock on the president's desk, opened the top drawer, inserted the pages, and closed it. Then he watched ten seconds elapse on his watch and retrieved the pages, now filled with text.

"Sino Super-Soldiers," the header read. "Chinese DNA Altering Update."

Doc's attention was instantly riveted to the pages, and he had difficulty believing what he read wasn't science fiction.

"Our intelligence sources on the ground in China have confirmed that a team of military doctors and scientists have made groundbreaking progress in experimental gene editing among Chinese military personnel," the summary began. "The latest progress reports indicate China has experienced significantly greater success in recent months with their experimental editing of human genes (laser DNA alteration) than American and allied scientists originally anticipated.

"Although the effort began just three years ago," the summary continued, "data obtained in recent days indicates China's gene-editing experiments are producing surprising progress toward its vision of stronger, faster soldiers who are better able to function under extreme weather conditions and chemical attacks."

The information sounded important enough, ominous even. But Doc wasn't at all sure what the implications might be for the free world ... and why the president insisted that he read it right away. He knew the team would have questions, and he had no good answers for them. So he decided to read the letter aloud to them before he called the president back.

"Questions?" Doc asked when he finished reading the paper to the team.

"What does it mean for our mission?" Louis asked.

"I haven't got the slightest idea," Doc told him. "But it sounds like we might run into soldiers who can rip our heads off with their bare hands instead of having to cut them off."

"That's not funny, Doc," Q told him. "If there's anything worse than a Chinese soldier, it's one that's stronger, faster, and harder to kill. And now we find out they actually exist."

"But our information says the program is still experimental," Jenny noted.

"True," Doc said. "So let's find out what the president thinks that means for us."

"We've read it, Mr. President," Doc said and set the speakerphone when the president took the call.

"Well, I know you all have questions. So let's hear 'em," the president said.

"What's the bottom line for us?" Q asked. "Are we going to have to slap a few of these so-called super-soldiers around? Or do we have your authorization to just shoot 'em on sight?"

"Relax, Q," the president laughed into the phone. "As far as we currently know, there's little chance that you'll encounter one of the test tube toy soldiers. As far as we know, there are only a few dozen of them housed at a Chinese military hospital on a remote base inside Nepal. But I wanted to be sure you at least knew about their existence."

"What are the doctors inflicting on those soldiers?" Jenny asked.

"We can only imagine, Jenny," the president said candidly. "I don't have to tell you what an authoritarian country the modern Peoples' Republic is. They don't ask for volunteers for efforts like this; they command participation. Given the nature of the experiments, it's a given that there have been many agonizing, probably fatal, dead ends. But that would have no bearing on China's determination to press on, no matter the cost in treasure and lives.

"The Reds are determined to exert their will throughout Asia and beyond. Enhancing the speed, strength, and resilience of its military forces would exponentially increase their chances of success. So it's really no surprise to us that they have increased their efforts. And now we know those efforts appear to be paying off sooner than any of our experts anticipated.

"So what does it mean for you and the rest of the team?" The president asked the obvious question. "Tread more lightly than usual out there. When you can, get word to the others about this just in case our experts have also misjudged how many robo-soldiers China's produced and where they are. Understood?"

"Understood, Mr. President," the team replied in unison.

"Godspeed, my friends!" the president said and ended the call.

On the *Dragon* that evening, the royals and Tuck ventured back into a dining car for supper, determined to mingle with the other passengers as much as was practical. Captain Michaels insisted that the SAS officers keep their distance, which they agreed to do with eyes-on at all times. Tuck was again overwhelmed by the crush of passengers who queued up to get a glimpse— and a photo or two—of the princess.

"I can't imagine what it must be like to be as photographed and gawked-at as you," Tuck told her sympathetically.

"After all these years, it's quite normal actually," the princess replied demurely. "It seems the least Marty and I can do for people who want nothing more than a moment to give a greeting or take a photo. It's a pittance to pay for the luxury of escaping isolation and feeling cloistered in this world filled with delightful people."

"But we all know from experience that they're not always 'delightful,'" Tuck replied. "And still, here you both are."

"My choice is simple, Tuck," the captain said cheerfully. "I go where the princess goes."

"Hear, hear!" Tuck said with his best-possible fake British accent.

The head attendant of the dining car staff gave the fawning passengers approximately ten minutes before quietly approaching the royals' table and reminding the crowd they had only half an hour to dine in order to ensure other passengers had the opportunity to enjoy a meal.

"Nicely done!" The captain commended the manager for his tact.

"Thank you ever so much," the princess softly told him with her best smile.

"My pleasure!" the manager replied. "And if you would be so kind, I would greatly appreciate having a photo taken with the two of you sometime before the end of the voyage."

"But of course! I was about to suggest it," the captain said. "We'll be sure to."

Supper went quietly over the next half-hour, with what seemed at the time to be a minor exception. While sipping from his glass of ice water, Tuck happened to notice a male attendant staring intently at him from a far corner. He dismissed it at first. But when he stole another glance, the attendant was still staring at him. Tuck was sure he hadn't interacted with the attendant. But it was clear the man was studying him.

Having a SAS officer accompany him when he exited the dining car made it easy for Tuck to escape the stranger's stare. But the retired naval officer was surprised to feel a little uneasy alone in his compartment. Moments later, while he washed his face and hands in the bathroom, he thought he heard two muffled taps on the door of his compartment. So he turned off the water and listened. He heard two more soft taps and checked the security monitor, and saw the attendant who had stared at him in the dining car pressed tight against the door.

"What is it you want?" he asked.

"Let me in, please!" the man pleaded urgently with a muffled voice. "I need your help!"

Tuck stood back from the door and weighed the circumstances. The attendant sounded desperate. His plea sounded eerily familiar to several he'd heard before from defectors seeking help to avoid capture. So he quietly unbolted the door and opened it.

"Thank you!" the man said with labored breath as he hurriedly slipped through the door.

"What can I do for you?" Tuck asked abruptly.

"Are you American?" the man asked and wiped the sweat from his forehead.

"You must know that from my accent," Tuck said incredulously.

"I didn't know any Americans were aboard until I heard you talking in the dining car," the man said. "Won't you please help me? I wish to defect from the Peoples' Republic of China. My name is—"

"I prefer not to know your name just yet," Tuck cut the man off. "But I *do* need to know why you've decided to defect and how you got on board."

"I am a second lieutenant in the People's Liberation Army," he explained. "I wish to go to America and alert your government about a program my country has underway to genetically alter its soldiers into incredibly strong but mindless killing machines. Please, sir," the young soldier pleaded. "You *must* help me. I have been on the run for days, and I'm exhausted. I must sleep. Won't you please at least let me sleep here tonight? I will move on in the morning if you wish, but tonight I must rest without fear of being discovered."

Tuck was surprised to learn the man was a soldier. He didn't look like one. He was stooped, and he limped. He had a slight curve to his back and a sunken chest. He might pass for an old, long-retired soldier, but certainly not one young and healthy enough for active duty. But Tuck had more urgent issues to deal with. He well understood the risk of harboring an AWOL Chinese soldier. And harboring him right under the noses of Chinese authorities was even riskier. The retired Navy captain had no doubt that his connection to the U.S. government meant that harboring a People's Liberation Army defector could get him jailed. Harboring one who knew Chinese military secrets could cost him his life.

But Tuck also knew that if what the soldier told him was true, the U.S. and its allies needed to hear it as soon as possible. So he threw caution to the wind, got a pillow and blanket from a cupboard, and pulled out the sleeper sofa in the sitting room. He knew he had to tell Doc of his predicament, but he waited until the soldier was asleep to make the call.

While he waited to hear the slow, steady sleeping breaths of the soldier, Tuck foraged for the pack of cigarettes he'd never unpacked from his favorite suitcase even though he'd quit smoking two decades ago. It would provide his plausible denial if he were discovered out on the tiny platform so late at night.

Half an hour later, he had Doc on the phone and told him about the AWOL soldier sleeping in his compartment … and that this particular defector had information the president needed to hear.

"I don't believe this!" Doc exclaimed. "You've got a defector sleeping with you!"

"That's not quite accurate," Tuck said in a weak attempt to lighten the conversation. "But he *is* asleep in my living room, and we're almost at the China-Nepal border. By morning, he will have escaped from China. And I thought you need to know that I will have helped him."

"But what makes him think he can ride with you all the way to London? It's not safe for him to stay with you for the whole trip, is it?" Doc asked the questions with no answers.

"It definitely won't be safe," Tuck replied. "But I don't see a safe alternative. I've seen enough of onboard security to know housekeeping will insist upon getting into my compartment before long. And I highly doubt they'll agree not to open my closet. If I knew when to expect them, I suppose our super-soldier could go for a brief walk."

"And if he's caught, can you count on him to keep his mouth shut?" Doc asked another question with no answer. "I mean, he's already told you he can't keep secrets."

"I don't see another way for him to make it to London safely, Doc," Tuck concluded. "I'd better end this call now. Wish me luck, and tell the president that tonight I just might be sleeping with the man who may help save the free world."

"That'll keep him awake for the next night or two," Doc chuckled nervously. "I'll update the others when they call in. Good night and good luck, Tuck. Call again when you can."

"Roger that," Tuck replied and turned his watch phone off, then headed to bed.

Tuck tossed and turned for an hour or so but eventually slipped into a restless sleep, fraught with nightmarish dreams of being chased from one end of the train to the other until he was finally caught, imprisoned, and shot. He awoke with a start a couple of times then drifted off again into another nightmare. He awoke for the fourth time at daybreak and forced himself to get out of bed. Halfway to the bathroom, he froze in his tracks. The soldier he'd let spend the night was gone. In his place, sound asleep, was a man Tuck had never seen before, sleeping like a baby. He looked much younger and healthier than the man Tuck had let spend the night.

"Get up!" he commanded the soldier.

"What? What time is it?" the soldier asked, half asleep.

"Don't worry about what time it is!" Tuck barked

irritably. "It's time to tell me who the hell you are and what happened to the other guy."

"What other guy?" the soldier asked sincerely.

"The other guy!" Tuck said more loudly and urgently. "The one I told he could spend the night. Did he let you in?"

Tuck saw a glint of remembrance in the soldier's eyes as the man bolted from the sofa and into the bathroom to look into the mirror.

"Oh, my god! I'm back!" the man said quietly. "I'm back!"

"Back?" Tuck asked incredulously. "You've never been here before!"

"No! I mean, I'm really back!" the soldier said loudly.

"Keep your voice down!" Tuck told him urgently. "I'm supposed to be alone."

"Yes," the soldier acknowledged. "I'm sorry to bring you such confusion. But I am the man you allowed to sleep here last night. Something important happened as I got a good night's rest. The muscles in my face relaxed, and I returned to my normal appearance."

"I don't understand," Tucks said, even more confused. "What are you talking about? What do you mean your face relaxed?"

"I was part of the army's gene-editing program. They administered lasers and injections that altered my body in terrible ways. I had spasms and other pain in waves, and I was unable to walk for days. Then one day, I discovered I had a new ability to manipulate the muscles in my face and completely change my appearance. I could look like someone else entirely."

"When you say you had the ability, do you mean you can do it at will?" Tuck asked.

"Exactly," the soldier told him. "I can't explain how I do it. But I have a new ability to manipulate my facial muscles in ways that change my appearance. It's like being able to wiggle my ears … except I have complete muscle control from ear to ear. Now it seems that while I am sleeping, my muscles can relax to the point of reverting to my original appearance."

"So this is the truth behind the stories we've heard in the U.S. about China's so-called super-soldier experiments," Tuck scoffed. "You can change your appearance? That hardly seems like much of a military advantage."

"It would be a great advantage if the enemy were looking for you, or if you had to elude facial recognition monitoring," the stranger told him.

"Can all the soldiers in the program do this?" Tuck asked.

"All of them," the soldier told him. "Some can also appear to be the opposite gender."

"Can you?" Tuck asked.

"Not yet," the stranger replied. 'But from what I have seen, that ability will come."

"And these changes happen at will? Do some take longer than others?" Tuck probed.

"Gene editing is gradual," the soldier explained. "But it ultimately alters the strength and flexibility of the body's four main tissues. At first, it changes the skin, then the muscles, then organs and nerves, and finally the bones, tendons, and ligaments."

"Can you do anything else that you couldn't before the program?" Tuck asked him.

"I can lift three times as much and run twice as fast," the soldier said. "Others have experienced even greater changes. Some can see three times as far. Others can go without sleep for days and not eat for a week or more without any discomfort or loss of energy. And we're all highly resistant to disease. The transformation is so complete, we call ourselves 'Edits'"

"It doesn't seem possible," Tuck said softly with a far-off look in his eye.

"That's what the world says about a mile-long train that travels at more than 400 miles per hour," the soldier said proudly. "But China is showing the world that man-made miracles are possible. Unfortunately for me and the other Edits who have been forced into the program, not all miracles are good. There are horrible side effects. Some Edits have muscles literally explode and rupture their skin like a shotgun blast. Still, others cannot deal with the often irreversible changes their bodies undergo. Some commit suicide to escape their unbearable physical and psychological pain.

"I considered suicide more than once during the four months I was subjected to the continual injections, tests, and observations. Finally, I knew I must escape, either by death or defection. I desperately wanted to defect to the United States, but I did not know how to do it. Hearing you speak was a miracle, and I knew I must take this chance and make my plea to you."

"But first, you had to board this train," Tuck concluded. "How did you manage that?"

"I paid an acquaintance to let me take his place on his new job as an attendant for this trip," the soldier explained. "He had already undergone all the necessary background checks, drug tests, and other screening. I merely altered my face to look like him and reported for work as one of the 120 attendants assigned to the *Dragon*. It was no more complicated than that."

"Unfortunately, it's the only part of this story that's easy to believe," Tuck said.

"However difficult my story is to believe, it is the truth," the soldier said.

"Are there other Edits onboard?" Tuck asked nervously.

"Two that I know of," the soldier told him. "They're pretending to be attendants too. And they've tracked me down and intend to drag me back to the Army to be punished for escaping. If you hadn't let me in last night, I'm sure they would have grabbed me by now."

"What names are they using?" Tuck asked.

"I don't know their names, but you can pick them out if you look closely," the soldier told him. "Their neck muscles are in near-constant motion. The movements are very subtle, but you can see them if you watch closely."

"Stay right here," Tuck told him. "I've gotta check in, but I'll be back soon."

Out onto the nearest platform, Tuck went and called Doc. The phone rang just once.

"What's up, Tuck?" Doc asked calmly.

"Doc," Tuck said slowly, "you won't guess in a million years what I'm about to tell you."

"There are Chinese super-soldiers onboard the train," Doc said flatly.

"How in the world do you know that?!" Tuck blurted out in frustration.

"Just an unlucky guess," Doc said with a sigh, a shrug, and a shake of his head. "How many are there?"

"The soldier I let into my compartment last night has only seen two others so far," Tuck told him. "But we can't be sure. Doc, you won't believe the things he says the Chinese military is putting soldiers through for the sake of creating better killing machines."

"Oh, I'd believe it, Tuck," Doc told him. "I've been briefed on this mad science, and I'm convinced the Reds are much darker than even Q makes them out to be."

"I've got to bring him in, don't I?" Tuck asked, knowing the answer.

"You know the president's going to want him on American soil," Doc said. "So do whatever it takes to bring him in. This is a tough call, Tuck, but I think it's wise not to advise Madeleine, Noah, and Rafe of this right now. We don't have the time on these calls to adequately explain the situation to each of them. And they're not able to help you hide this guy. So I don't want to add to the stress they're already under. It's one less lie they have to tell if they are questioned. Now we better end this call so you can get back and keep an eye on him."

"Roger that!" Tuck said and ended the call and hurried back to his compartment.

But when he arrived, the stranger was gone.

11

MOTHER OF SATAN

The following morning, Rafe had been on the treadmill in the fitness car for nearly half an hour when he spotted two members of the Chinese security force in the large mirror on the wall in front of him. When he realized they were walking in his direction, he braced himself and pretended not to see them until they stopped beside his treadmill.

"Bonjour!" he calmly said and stopped jogging.

"Good morning," one of them replied sternly, then held up a work ID badge and said, "I am Security Chief Chen Lo. I wonder if you may have seen this man in the last twelve hours?"

"No, I don't believe I have," Rafe replied honestly. "Why do you ask?"

"He is a member of the dining car staff and did not report for work yesterday or today," the officer said.

"Maybe he's not feeling well," Rafe suggested.

"He is not in his compartment," the officer said. "He does not respond when paged, and his co-workers have not seen him since supper was served on the day we departed Shanghai. We are concerned regarding his whereabouts. If you happen to see him, please tell him to contact his supervisor immediately."

"I'll be happy to," Rafe said. "What's his name? Do you think something may have happened to him?"

"His name is Jin Rai," the officer replied. "I'm certain there is a simple explanation. He's a new employee. Perhaps he is simply confused with his schedule. Sorry to have interrupted your workout. Thank you for your time."

"No problem, sir. I needed the break," Rafe told him. "Good luck in your search."

As Rafe began jogging again, questions ran through his mind.

How does someone vanish on a moving train? he asked himself. *Did he disappear on his own, or are others involved? Could this somehow be connected to a threat to the* Dragon?

For the first time since the *Dragon* left Shanghai, Rafe's gut told him a serious threat might be afoot. Intrigue had shown up. Danger was lurking not far behind. And the warrior shifted into battle mode. After his workout, he showered and headed to the dining car for fresh fruit, a couple of poached eggs, dry sprouted rye toast, tomato juice, and water. Grateful to have found a window table, he got comfortable and enjoyed the beauty of the snow-capped Hindu Kush Mountains in the distance as the *Dragon* crossed into southern Afghanistan.

The spectacle briefly held his attention but lost it when Mei Yin appeared at his table.

"Good morning, Monsieur Saint-Pallet!" she told him happily. "Aren't the mountains beautiful in the bright morning sun?"

"Oh, good morning to you, Mei Yin!" Rafe replied with a broad smile. "Yes, they are. What a great way to enjoy breakfast. I'm extremely pleased to see so much beauty on this trip!"

Catching his compliment, Mei Yin blushed, and her smile grew from formal to genuine.

"Can I get you anything more before you finish your meal?" she asked dutifully.

"No, I'm fine, thank you!" he replied and warmly held her gaze for an extra moment. "Are you enjoying your job so far?" he asked to keep her at the table a little longer.

"I am, very much!" she told him. "How about you? Are you enjoying the trip? Are you finding interesting things to write about and photograph?"

"That I am, Mei Yin," he replied. "And you've given me

an idea. Sometime in the next few days, I would very much like to take some group photographs of the entire dining car staff. Do you think you might be able to help me make the necessary arrangements?"

"I would be happy to!" she told him with an even brighter smile. "But I really must get back to work. Enjoy the rest of your meal and have a wonderful day, Monsieur Saint-Pallet!"

"And you as well, Mei Yin," he said and watched her walk across the dining car and enter the kitchen.

The next thought he had was of the missing dining attendant, Jin Rai. He wondered if security had located the young man yet, and if so, where. It was a curious development on a trip that had so far been a pleasant procession of great meals and interesting people, the most interesting being Mei Yin.

As Rafe held that thought, a well-dressed, distinguished-looking older gentleman stopped at the table.

"How do you do, Monsieur Saint-Pallet," the gentleman said softly and bowed slightly. "My name is Zhang Yong Lǐ. I am privileged to serve as chief design engineer of this miracle machine that has become known as the *Dragon*. What do you think of her so far, if I may ask?"

"It's a pleasure to meet you, Mr. Lǐ," Rafe said sincerely. "Speaking as a passenger, I think the *Dragon* is absolutely perfect!" Rafe told him honestly.

"I am very happy to hear that," the engineer replied. "And as an experienced and widely traveled travel writer, what do you think of her?"

"I think she's every bit as perfect," Rafe told him in his most convincing tone.

"That is wonderful to hear!" the engineer said happily. "It relieves me of any anxiety about asking that you please be as kind as you are thorough in your assessment of the *Dragon* in the articles you write about this voyage."

"Oh, I can assure you that my coverage will be highly complementary." Rafe stretched the truth in order to capitalize on this fortunate encounter with the person he most wanted to talk to about the *Dragon*. "I had no idea you were on board. I'm thrilled to have this unexpected opportunity to speak to the most knowledgeable person about the engineering, imagination, and innovation that went into making the *Dragon* the miracle machine that it is."

"I'm flattered to hear the *Dragon* receive such high praise from you, Monsieur Saint-Pallet," Mr. Li gushed. "And I will gladly provide you with whatever information I can. When can we begin?"

"How about right now?" Rafe asked.

"I would like nothing better!" the engineer said cheerfully.

"I wonder if you wouldn't mind if the American, Mr.

Baird, joins us," Rafe asked, purposely avoiding the mention of Tuck's military rank. "I happened to meet him yesterday, and he went on and on about his love of trains ... especially the *Dragon*. He would love this!"

"I'd like nothing better!" the engineer said. "Please give him a call and let me know when you both are ready."

Moments later, Tuck was hustling to join the pair in the dining car.

"Lead the way!" Rafe said to the engineer when Tuck arrived. "I have a small recorder. Do you mind if I use it?"

"Please do, by all means!" the engineer told him.

"The magazine called your staff a week prior to our departure to confirm there would be a photographer along on this trip. I'm afraid I'm not as good with photos as I am with words."

"Liu Wei is our excellent staff photographer," the engineer told him and made the call.

For the next hour and a half, the four of them wandered from one end of the *Dragon* to the other while Rafe and Tuck peppered the engineer with technical questions about every aspect of the engineering wonder. They concluded the tour in the *Dragon's* small media library, where passengers could borrow DVDs and books or enjoy them in one of six cubicles.

Rafe cautiously asked, "Now that we know the basics

about all this remarkable train's strengths, what can you tell us about her weaknesses?"

"She has none," the engineer shot back proudly.

Rafe pressed him for answers. "Everything ever created by man has weaknesses."

"Not the *Dragon!*" the engineer replied and stuck his chest out. "She's perfect!"

"A man named Thomas Andrews once said pretty much the same thing about one of his creations," Rafe told him.

"Didn't Thomas Andrews design the *Titanic*?" Tuck blurted out.

"Yes, he did. And he's the one who told the world she was unsinkable," Rafe explained. "He was sure of it right up until he went down with her after leading as many passengers as he could to lifeboats. So please think, Mr. Li," Rafe pressed a little more gently, "what's the *Dragon's* Achille's heel? If terrorists wanted to cripple or destroy her, how might they do it? Would they attack her mag-lev technology? Her universal rail gauge system? Her computers?"

Mr. Li leaned against a rack of Blu-ray discs and silently thought for a few moments.

"You're not really a travel writer, are you, Monsieur Saint-Pallet?" Mr. Li asked Rafe with a small, knowing smile. "And you're more than just a close friend of the royals, aren't you, Mr. Baird?" he asked Tuck.

"You answer my question, and we'll answer yours," Rafe promised.

"Follow me," the engineer said with an intense look.

The engineer strode with a new urgency and marched the pair through the sliding double security doors to the center of the second car to a vacant twelve-foot-square space between the computer compartment at the front of the car and the security command post at the rear.

"Are there no security measures in place to lock and unlock these doors?" Tuck asked in stunned disbelief.

"Of course," the engineer told him. "I carry a fob that disables the locks of all security doors when I approach them. The doors then relock automatically if I move more than three feet away from them.

"Nice," Tuck replied and made a mental note for Noah. "Who else has fobs?"

"All security and military personnel on board," the engineer told him matter-of-factly and continued his explanation. "This space was incorporated into the design because we anticipated an occasional need to securely transport bulky and valuable cargo," the engineer explained. "The large doors on either side serve as ramps for loading and unloading. If I were intent on disabling—and then destroying—the *Dragon*, I would place explosives here and in the identical space at the rearward end of the car in front of the rear lead car. Enough of the right kind of explosives would sever the *Dragon's* heads at both ends. The center cars—and the passengers within—would be at the mercy of the terrorists. But as you can see, there are no explosives here."

Rafe raised a finger to his lips thoughtfully while his eyes scanned the empty space. "Since the *Dragon* began her journey, I've marveled at how quiet she is. How did you achieve such an amazingly quiet interior, even in this wide open, unoccupied space?"

"Well, it all starts with the ultra-quiet mag-lev technology—" the engineer began.

"But there has to be more to it," Rafe interrupted him, "because she's equally quiet right now in southern Afghanistan, clanking along on metal wheels at a little more than 100 kilometers per hour, rolling over 1,520 millimeter-gauge tracks … the narrowest and noisiest in the world."

"I was right, Monsieur Saint-Pallet," the engineer coyly stated. "You are much more than a travel writer. We devised a groundbreaking insulation system with state-of-the-art sound-deadening properties."

"Could I see it?" Rafe asked on a hunch.

"Of course!" Mr. Li said proudly and showed Rafe and Tuck how easy it was to remove a lightweight, carbon-fiber, floor-to-ceiling wall panel.

Behind it, laid-in like a giant slice of cheese was a foil-wrapped, hermetically sealed, foam-filled pad measuring eight inches thick and four feet wide by eight feet high."

"What's behind that insulation?" Tuck asked the engineer.

"The ... outer ... wall," the engineer said slowly, puzzled by what he saw.

"Why did you say it like that?" Rafe probed.

"This insulation is wrong," the engineer said.

"What do you mean?" Tuck asked.

"The foil encasement is wrong," Mr. Li replied. "It's not pleated as we specified, and it appears to be thinner."

Rafe bent at the waist, pulled a nine-inch stiletto switchblade from his right boot, and opened it with a firm click.

"The average travel writer doesn't carry a weapon like that," Mr. Li said.

"This?" Rafe asked and held the knife in front of him. "It was a gift from Mr. Omar Keller, a Swiss cutlery representative I happened to meet last night."

"But passengers are not permitted to have weapons on board," Mr. Li reminded him.

"To a cutlery sales representative, this is a 'utensil,'" Rafe told him and cut a small slit in the insulation.

"Whoa! What are you doing?" Mr. Li exclaimed as Rafe stuck a little finger into the slit and then into his mouth.

Rafe held up a hand to signal he needed a moment before answering, then again stuck his little finger into the slit and into his mouth.

"What on earth are you tasting?" Mr. Li asked incredulously. "It's foam, not powder!"

"TATP," Rafe said to Tuck ominously.

"What?" Mr. Li demanded a better answer.

"Tri-cyclic acetone peroxide," Rafe replied. "Mother of Satan!"

"But why did the onboard explosive detectors not alert us?" Mr. Li thought out loud.

"It must have something to do with the foil wrapper it's sealed within," Tuck deduced. "Is the entire train wrapped in this insulation?"

"God forgive me, it is!" Mr. Li gasped.

"Houston, we have a problem..." Tuck said softly and rubbed the back of his neck.

"Who are you talking to?" the frantic engineer asked.

"It's an American expression to say there's enough explosive onboard to blow us all to hell and back," Rafe explained with dark humor.

"We have to get the passengers off this train!" Mr. Li nearly shouted.

"Whoa! Let's think this through," Rafe told him. "Whoever intends to set this stuff off has a plan. If they even begin to suspect we're on to them, their plan goes out the window, and they might pull the plug right then and there."

"So what do you suggest we do?" Mr. Li asked in desperation.

"Liu Wei, I would appreciate photos of this insulation and then, if you please, give us a few moments alone," he asked the photographer. "Then we'll put the wall panel back."

"But we must do something about the explosive!" Mr. Li said urgently.

"Stay calm, Mr. Li," Rafe told him. "I know how concerned you must be for the passengers—and for the *Dragon*—but I believe we're safe for the next several hours."

"How can you say that with any certainty?" Mr. Li challenged him.

"There's nothing between here and the Iran border, and well into Iran's interior. Am I correct in thinking that the *Dragon* can't go faster than this until at least this time tomorrow?"

"Perhaps even a bit longer, depending on the weather," Mr. Li confirmed.

"Well, that gives us time to get some important answers and come up with a plan of our own," Rafe said with a trace of relief. "That is, if we can trust the crew that's driving this thing."

"I believe we can," Mr. Li said with certainty. "They were selected at the very last minute from among China's most accomplished crew members. But we have to at least alert onboard security," Mr. Li insisted.

"I'm not so sure that would be wise," Tuck told him.

"But why not?" the engineer asked incredulously.

"The same security force was in charge while the *Dragon* was assembled, was it not?" Tuck asked him.

"Yes, of course," the engineer replied.

"Well, there's a traitorous breach in that security," Tuck told him. "How else did this entire train get lined with TATP?"

"I suppose you're right," the engineer said and sagged in surrender. "But that leaves us little hope of survival."

"Fortunately, that's where you're wrong, Mr. Li!" Tuck told him and put a hand on the engineer's stooped shoulder. "The safety of this machine and everyone on board is of paramount concern to many far beyond China's borders. Trust me when I say that those in the highest authority in a number of powerful capitols around the world are every bit as invested as your government in the safety and success of this journey. That's all I can share with you for now. I hope it's enough to give you some peace of mind."

"I suppose you're right," the engineer said with a slightly better grasp of the sort of men who were with him in that moment. "And I trust you'll do what's right," he said sincerely.

"You have our word, Mr. Li," Rafe said. "And we must have your word that you won't speak to anyone else on board about this before the three of us get back together."

"You have my word," Mr. Li agreed. "But I must alert President Chen."

"And we've gotta call Doc, Tuck," Rafe said.

"Who's Doc, and how do you both know him?" Mr. Li asked, more puzzled than ever.

"He's another fella you can trust with your life," Tuck told him as he and Rafe headed to the nearest outside platform to make the call.

PARIS WAS STILL MORE THAN SIX THOUSAND MILES AWAY. And Nostradamus was roaming her bars, back streets, and alleys hoping to hear some mumblings about Alexandre Rafael Bellarose, the French Foreign Legionnaire who got him locked away in that stinking

Paris prison. He cryptically asked the few shadowy characters he spoke with whether they'd heard of any French train accidents recently, but they couldn't help him. And then, about midday, a tipsy fellow sitting on a stoop two doors down from a small, dingy bar told him a jumbled, convoluted story about a legionnaire named Alexandre Bellarose had saved the life of a fellow legionnaire, Gabriel Chastain, who was France's greatest living hero. But the poor drunkard had no clue where either of the heroes might be.

And so it went until well after dark when the madman headed back to the area where he'd encountered Genevieve Valoir the night before. His motives were selfish. Even after having rescued her, it wasn't her safety that sent him in her direction. Rather, he hoped that seeing her again would calm his heart and mind as it had the first time. He needed to see her so badly he didn't bother with pretense. He didn't have the time or energy to disguise his return as a coincidence.

So he simply waited on a bench on the block where they'd met the night before and hoped she would soon appear. He didn't have to wait long. The sound of her happy walk on the cobblestones lifted the madman's heart, and he began to feel better even before she appeared.

"Hello again, milady!" Nostradamus said with a smile as he stood and bowed. "I'd hoped you might still walk this way and that we might meet again."

"Well, hello!" Genevieve said with a smile. "I'm happy to

see you again. I feared I might never have another chance to properly thank you for coming to my rescue. I am most grateful."

"Grateful enough to allow me to walk you home?" he asked hopefully.

"I suppose I might like that, despite your oddness," Genevieve said with a smile.

"What do you find so odd about me?" Nostradamus asked earnestly.

"Your insistence that you are Nostradamus defies logic and science," she chuckled.

"What do logic and science offer when compared to the clear evidence that I stand here, before your very eyes?" He met her challenge with one of his own.

"But science and logic are the evidence that assertions such as yours require," she told him more seriously.

"Perhaps that's true in your world," he conceded. "But it's not true in mine."

"And where is *your* world, exactly?" she probed in the hope of progress.

"You are walking through it as we speak, milady," the madman replied.

"If this is your world, where is mine?" she probed him further.

"While you are in my world, there's no need for yours," he answered.

"But I live in my world, and you have offered to walk me home," she reminded him.

"Well then, it could take some time to get there," he said. "And that's just fine with me."

"But I am tired after a long, challenging shift," she sighed. "So I really must get home."

"Where do you work?" he asked her, finally.

"Paris Aide Santé Mentale," she told him as casually as she could.

"That sounds like interesting work," he said simply. "What do you do there?"

"I'm a cognitive psychologist," she said more directly.

"*Really*!?!" He stopped walking and asked with great surprise.

"Well, don't act so surprised," Genevieve told him. "I'm smarter than I appear to be."

"Oh, I meant no offense," the madman assured her and fell in step with her again. "My surprise is merely that you have chosen such a challenging vocation."

"It can be challenging at times, for sure," she agreed. "But it's supremely rewarding."

"I'm certain of that," her companion agreed. "You must have opportunities to help some very deserving people."

"I do, at that," she said softly. "And I would like to help you if you would allow me to."

"Me?" he asked with his greatest surprise. "How might you be able to help me?"

"I should think it must be very awkward being Nostradamus in the twenty-first century," she stated matter-of-factly.

"Awkward for others, perhaps," he hesitantly conceded. "But never for me ... except ..."

"Go on," she encouraged her new friend to complete his thought.

"I do lose track of time and place now and then," he admitted.

"What is that like?" the psychologist in her wanted to know.

"The best I can explain it is that it's like falling asleep on a bus and missing your stop, and then awakening to realize you have no idea what time it is or where you are," he told her.

"So you experience blackouts," she told him calmly.

"I guess you could call them that," he answered. "I don't give them much thought."

"You don't?" she asked in surprise. "Doesn't it worry you

that you completely lose touch with the world around you? Doesn't that leave you at the mercy of harmful circumstances and people you may not even know?"

"Like I said, I don't give it much thought," he said with a slight edge in his voice.

"Would you be willing to turn around and go to the hospital with me?" she asked.

"I suppose so," he answered slowly, "if you would be willing to help me with a dream I recently had."

"Of course!" she answered as she took his arm and turned him toward the hospital. "Tell me about it, please, as we go."

"I dreamed that a good friend of mine was riding aboard a beautiful, huge, space-age train in some far-off place, traveling at insanely fast speeds," he told her.

"Well, it's quite interesting so far," she said. "Can you tell me anything more?"

"He was surrounded by people of many cultures, speaking many different languages," he continued. "But they all seemed to be going to the same place. Can you make any sense of that?"

"Can you describe the train better, or perhaps guess what country it was in?" she asked.

"I'm afraid I cannot," the madman sighed. "I've racked my brain but haven't a clue."

Genevieve was silently surprised to learn that the man on her arm was so out of touch with the big news that China had unveiled the *Dragon* to the world some time ago and that it was due in Paris in less than a week, bringing with it a couple of hundred passengers from at least a dozen countries. But she resisted the urge to tell him because she feared he might run off if she gave him the information he was looking for. And her goal now was to get him to the hospital.

R afe and Tuck squeezed onto the nearest outside platform and called Doc.

"What's the latest?" Doc asked intently without the formality of a greeting.

"As you say in America, we're up to our asses in alligators, Doc," Rafe said plainly.

"Have you identified more Edits?" Doc asked, forgetting what Rafe didn't know.

"What?" Rafe shot back. "What are you talking about?"

"Sorry, Rafe," Doc said sincerely. "I told Tuck not to tell you about the Edits. We'll bring you up to speed in a minute. But first, why did you call?"

"The *Dragon's* wearing a Mother of Satan overcoat," Rafe said flatly.

"What?!" Doc practically shouted urgently. "What are you saying?"

"You heard me," Rafe said plainly. "Tuck and I toured the *Dragon* with the chief design engineer, and we discovered that the entire fuselage is wrapped in TATP-laced insulation. Whoever installed it can blow it—and us—to high heaven at will."

"Oh, Christ, Rafe!" Doc grunted. "Please tell me that's a very bad joke."

"I'd love to, but I'm serious as a heart attack, to use another American phrase," Rafe said.

"Is Tuck there with you?" Doc asked urgently.

"I'm right here, Doc!" Tuck replied just as urgently.

"Call me, and I'll call Q, Jenny, and Louis," Doc said. "We need them on this call, too."

The six of them were almost instantly on a secure satellite call.

"Can everyone hear okay?" Doc asked.

"Loud and clear!" Q shot back, like the others.

"Okay, Tuck and Rafe, let's hear about the Mother of Satan," Doc said.

"Mother of Satan?" Q exclaimed. "There's TATP on that train?"

"Easy, Q," Doc said calmly into the phone. "If you don't

pace yourself, this call will send you into cardiac arrest before it's over. How much would you say there is, Rafe?"

"Enough to send the *Dragon* and everyone on board to the moon," Rafe estimated.

"That's a lot of explosive," Louis noted. "Where did they hide it, and how did they manage to get it on board?"

"That's 'the tell' in all this," Tuck interjected. "There's more here than anyone would ever guess, and it's in the very last place anyone would ever look. It's in the sound-dampening foam insulation panels in the outer walls throughout the train. So the plot originated before assembly even began ... which means it's bigger than the Red Z."

"So now's a good time to discuss the Edits onboard and what, if anything, you think they might have to do with all this," Doc told the retired Navy captain.

"Edits?" Q nearly shouted. "What the hell are Edits?"

"Chinese super-soldiers," Tuck answered, "They call themselves Edits because their genes are edited. We've known for more than a decade that Chinese military scientists were experimenting with human genome editing technologies. We also knew they've made progress at altering soldiers' DNA, making changes in physical traits, like eye color and disease resistance.

"But night before last, I was approached by an Edit who's able to radically change his facial features and physical stature. He told me he can lift three times more weight and run twice as fast as he could before his treatments began. He says many Edits can go without sleep or food for days without discomfort or loss of energy.

"He snuck aboard in Shanghai," Tuck added. "He approached me when he heard my Yankee accent and told me he plans to defect to the States and blow the whistle on the program."

"But why?" Jenny asked flatly and skeptically.

"He says Edits all suffer with severe headaches and muscle spasms. Some have muscles literally explode and rupture their skin."

"Where is this chucklehead now?" Q asked angrily.

"He gave me the slip and is hiding somewhere to avoid being caught by two other Edits he believes are on board," Tuck said apologetically. "I don't know his name or the names or whereabouts of the other two either. He did say they can be identified by subtle, uncontrollable neck muscle movements. We need to find them soon. But to tell you the truth, when Rafe and I got the unexpected opportunity to tour the *Dragon* from end to end and then discovered the Mother of Satan, that took priority."

"So who put the TATP in place?" Doc prodded the team.

"Believe me," Rafe answered, "it took hundreds of hands and hours. And it took untold hours and resources to manufacture the insulation and get everyone security clearances for everyone who installed it. There's no way the Red Z has the wherewithal to pull all that off."

"Well, there's also no way the Chinese government is behind this," Tuck said with certainty. "There's no upside for them. Why fake a hijacking and hold the *Dragon* and Britain's princess hostage to spark international unrest? Why invest all the planning and expense of making this journey a reality only to blow the princess and the *Dragon* to smithereens on the very trip they conceived to promote its reliability and safety."

"I'd say that leaves the military as the only possible co-conspirators," Louis concluded.

"The Red Z may have allied with a radical faction within the People's Liberation Army," Jenny suggested. "Using Red Z frontmen would give the PLA plausible deniability while fomenting war by threatening a massacre far outside China's borders."

The team went dead silent for a few seconds before Doc finally said, "I think we're very close to the truth, here, team. But it all hangs on one question we haven't asked yet. What's the plan for the Mother of Satan?"

"It's rigged to be detonated remotely," Rafe answered. "I'm sure of it."

"Why are you so sure?" Doc challenged him.

"It was strategically and painstakingly installed behind

all the wall panels," Rafe said. "Setting one off remotely would trigger all the rest right on down the line."

"A remote detonator rules out a suicide mission," Doc figured. "So we know they plan to show themselves and hold the *Dragon* hostage at a stop. But which one?"

"Well, that's a crapshoot for sure," Q mumbled.

"I need to get the president in the loop," Doc told them. "Sit tight, everyone, until I have more for you. Rafe, get back to that engineer and start figuring out how to jam the detonator signal. If this all suddenly goes south, we don't want whoever has the detonator to go out with a bang and take everyone else along. Tuck, get busy finding that super-soldier and the two other ones who are hunting him. My gut tells me they may have Red Z ties.

"Louis and Jenny, start packing because I'm sure the president's going to want you closer to London. And Rafe, tell Noah or Madeleine to call me, and I'll take it from there. Q, don't run off. I want you on the call with the president. That's it for now, team. Thank you for the great work. Now get back to it."

"I'm still on the line, Doc," Q assured his friend once everyone else had hung up. "I just ordered pastis and tapenade at a cozy sidewalk café. This has been a great mission so far. But I've got a feeling you're about to put an end to that."

"You know I'm going to tell Marsha about the pastis," Doc chuckled. "I'm calling the White House now, and it will likely take your pal the president a few minutes to come on the line. So sit tight and don't burp."

"Roger that!" Q said simply and put his feet up on the empty chair at his table.

"Hello, to my two favorite desperadoes!" the president boomed when he took the call. "I understand the *Dragon* is making amazing time somewhere in central Turkey. She's on time to be nearing Sarajevo in about twenty-four hours. Then she's less than another twenty-four hours from Paris. So what good news have you got for me?"

"Well, Mr. President, we've found explosives," Doc said as directly as possible.

"What explosives?" the president boomed louder than ever before on the phone.

"According to Tuck and the chief design engineer, the entire train is wrapped in a layer of sound-deadening insulation that's impregnated with TATP," Doc told him. "Their guess is that one of the panels is rigged to be detonated remotely, which will trigger a chain reaction that will completely destroy the *Dragon*."

"Well, Doc, you just pooped in my punch bowl," the president sighed. "Do we have any idea where the detonator is and how they plan to use it?"

"We don't have a clue where it is," Doc answered. "But our best guess is that they plan to hijack the *Dragon* before it reaches England and de-board the passengers from nations allied with China. Then they can threaten to blow up the *Dragon*, the princess, and the other remaining passengers unless their demands are met. Whether they blow it up or not, they will have created a tinderbox powerful enough to spark an international conflict and propel China into a more aggressive, more dominant role globally.

"That makes so much sense, I fear you're right," the president replied.

"So if you were a betting man, Mr. President—and I know you're not—but if you were, what stop would you bet they'll make their move at?" Q asked.

"Paris," the president said immediately.

"What makes you so sure?" Doc asked with more than a little surprise.

"They've almost completely transited the 'Silk Road,' gentleman," the president told them. "With the exception of some minor hiccups, China's been on very good terms with all the kingdoms and countries between Nepal and Turkey for more than two hundred years. The terrorists behind this plot know better than to try anything that might upset that applecart."

"But that still leaves the stops scheduled for Sarajevo and Zurich before Paris," Doc said.

"Not if we shut them down," the president said. "If my hunch is right and we eliminate those two stops, France is all they have left because they won't dare let the

Dragon take them to England. Leaving the continent would reduce their odds of escaping to almost zero."

"How will we explain not stopping in Sarajevo and Zurich?" Doc asked.

"We can announce an outbreak of a particularly vicious strain of flu virus or some other contagion," the president thought out loud. "We only need a cover story long enough to keep the train rolling toward Paris. Odds are the terrorists plan to hijack the *Dragon* outside Paris, most likely in or around a relatively small town like Créteil. And we've got to be ready for it."

"What about the crew?" Doc asked. "How many crew members are there? How do we know we can trust them all?"

Doc, your team on the *Dragon* must find that detonator and neutralize it. I don't know how. I don't care how. Neutralizing the Mother of Satan ends the nightmare of no survivors. Then you just face the nightmare of a gunfight to save the passengers."

China's President Xiu Ying Chen must have been alerted by now. I wonder what's taking him so long to call me," the president said. "He knows we have Tuck aboard … and you better believe he suspects we have others along for the ride. I'm going to have Louis and Jenny join you and Doc in Paris. If this deteriorates into a standoff, we're not going to stand by and hope the Chinese handle it.

"I want the four of you to pull out all the stops, be in

constant contact with Tuck, Rafe, Madeleine, and Noah and do whatever is necessary to ensure the princess is safe. If you can also save the *Dragon*, that will help me smooth President Chen's feathers because he's going to go through the roof when you insert your team, Doc."

"We'll do our best, as always, Mr. President," Doc assured him.

"I know you will, Doc," the president said. "I'm just talking to calm myself down."

"Whoa!" Q suddenly blurted into his phone. "Hold the bus! You're not going to believe this, but Chastain just walked right by the café with some dame."

"What?" Doc asked in disbelief. "No way! He's in prison in …"

"In Paris," the president finished Doc's sentence.

"Well, call President DuPris, Mr. President," Q said sarcastically, "because one of the steers has wandered off the ranch and is headed north on Place d'Estienne d'Orves as we speak … with quite a looker on his arm, if I do say so myself. And don't tell Marsha I said that, Doc."

"Are you sure it's Chastain, Q?" Doc asked.

"Sure as I'm sitting here eating smashed olives and sardines," Q shot back. "He's trying to hide under a hoodie, but I know that face. We fought for our lives shoulder-to-shoulder with Chastain in that downed chopper near Sedona, Arizona, just over two years ago, Doc. I don't forget that sort of thing."

"I'll call DuPris, fellas," the president said with a happier tone. "I'm sure he's got all of Paris looking for Chastain, and I need to give somebody good news. What's the cross street, Q?"

"Rue d'Clichy," Q replied. "I guess that's how you say it. My French sucks, I know."

"It's close enough, Q. Thanks!" the president said happily. "I gotta call DuPris and Prime Minister Elliott with the news. Call me if anything more hits the fan."

"Roger that, Mr. President!" Doc and Q said and waited for the president to hang up.

With the call over, Q followed Chastain at a distance. Jenny and Louis began packing. Rafe headed back to rejoin Mr. Li and help him figure a scheme to defeat the remote detonator. Tuck pondered the fate of the Edit, who was calling himself Jin Rai, and the two nameless Edits who were also trying desperately to find the missing dining car attendant. The retired Navy captain knew he also needed to reunite with his friend, Captain Michaels, and the princess. He knew they needed to hear about the craziness unfolding on the train from him before they heard about it from London. So he called his old friend and requested that he and the princess join him for a nighttime tea before calling it a day.

"Hello, Marty!" Tuck said as cheerfully as he could when

his friend took the call. "I know it's late, but I can't seem to unwind. I was hoping I could persuade you and the princess to join me for a late-night tea in Dining Car Two. I really need a cup to relax me."

"Of course!" the British captain replied. "I'm sure Mary would love to. She hasn't slept for more than four hours a night on this trip. The *Dragon* has taken her back to her childhood, and she just wants to take in every possible moment while it lasts. Go on ahead and order the tea. We'll join you shortly."

Rafe found Mr. Li on the phone talking to his technical support team back in Shanghai about the challenge of locating the detonator circuit among two miles of insulating foam. He wasn't happy when he ended the call.

"Well, what did you find out?" Rafe asked as optimistically as he could.

"Your friend was right," Mr. Li sighed heavily. "We do indeed have a terrible problem."

"Which is?" Rafe pressed the question.

"My team fears this TATP could be too unstable for us to examine closely," the anguished engineer said. "They feel it's extremely risky to even scan the insulation with a metal detector. The fear is that an electromagnetic field strong enough to detect the components of a detonator embedded in the foam might be strong enough to set it off."

"Can we be confident that they will not leak word of this to the media until we have overcome this threat?" Rafe asked.

"We can, I'm sure of it," Mr. Li said confidently. "China's honor is at stake."

"That's good to hear," Rafe told him with a bit of relief. "Now, let's focus. We know our enemy has created a fail-safe killing machine," he said. "So we've got to find the detonator. You're familiar with the crew and attendants on board, Mr. Li. Where would you start looking?"

"I'm afraid I have no better guess than you, Monsieur Saint-Pallet," the engineer sighed. "So I will follow your lead. What would you have me do?"

"Early this morning, your security people were looking for a missing dining room attendant named Jin Rai who hasn't reported to work for the last two days," Rafe told him. "But he approached my friend, Mr. Baird, the day before yesterday and said he's an AWOL Chinese soldier and intends to defect to the United States when we reach London. He said two Chinese undercover agents are on board searching for him because he's fleeing a top-secret military program.

"Security may already have him in custody, and if any part of his story is true, it's the oddest story unfolding on this train. So I'd appreciate your following up with security to see if they've located him ... and if they have, perhaps he was carrying the detonator. In the meantime, I'll keep looking for the two agents he claimed to be hiding from. My guess is that the detonator will be with one of those three characters. Here's my cell number. Call me with whatever you find out."

"Will do," Mr. Li said dutifully and headed toward the security post.

WHILE RAFE AND MR. LI SET OUT TO FIND THE detonator as the *Dragon* raced across Turkey, Q hustled into the Paris night to keep Chastain in view as the streets began to empty and grow dark. It was obvious Chastain was focused on the attractive lady on his arm, so Q followed much closer behind the pair than he normally would have and listened in on their conversation.

"So why are we going to the hospital?" Chastain asked his companion. "Your shift is over, and it's late. Aren't you tired?"

"I am," Genevieve admitted. "But we really must get to the bottom of your blackouts, and I need to know you are in a safe environment and available as we work to discover the cause. It's not at all practical—and a little unsafe—for you to be roaming the streets and telling people you are Nostradamus."

"But that is who I am!" Chastain reasoned. "What other name would I give them?"

"What other name do you have?" the psychologist asked, hoping to spark a memory.

"Gabriel …" he said reflexively.

"Just Gabriel?" she prodded him. "Have you no last name?"

"Just Gabriel," he told her simply.

"Like the angel?" she continued prodding.

"*Hardly!*" he shot back at her.

"Why do you say it like that?" she prodded him more.

"No man is an angel," he told her solemnly, "least of all me."

"That is where you are wrong," she told him with a beautiful smile. "All men are quite capable of being angels in the best and worst of times, and I have a good feeling about you."

She hailed an orderly as she and Chastain entered the sliding emergency room doors of the hospital and personally signed him in so that she could ensure he got the help he needed.

13

By that time, Tuck was in the midst of laughs and light conversation with Princess Mary and his old friend, Captain Michaels, while they enjoyed hot tea and the full moon that illuminated the mountain ridges of Western Turkey in the windows of their dining car.

"I'm not sorry you can't sleep, Tuck," the princess said demurely. "I am glad to finally have some quiet time with just the three of us. How are you enjoying the trip so far?"

"Believe me, Mary, it's been beyond my wildest dreams," Tuck said as cryptically as he could manage. "The *Dragon* is truly a wondrous machine, built for the modern age. So tell me, do you think it's right for Great Britain?"

"I do," she answered with confident excitement. "As you know, I've looked it over extensively, and the quality and attention to detail are obvious everywhere. But even more important, the speed and comfort it delivers are all that I had hoped for. A fleet of *Dragons* would reduce travel times between London and cities like Glasgow, Dublin, and Paris by more than half and accommodate more than twice as many passengers. And you just know that the engineering and technology breakthroughs that have made such a train possible have to mean greater safety."

Tuck almost dribbled his tea down his chin when he heard that last vote of confidence.

"I commend you for your commitment to ensure Britons enjoy the best mass transit the twenty-first century has to offer," Tuck told her diplomatically. "But given the complexity of the train's software and mechanical engineering, you can never be too careful in reaching a decision to invest in such an expensive leap forward."

What he wanted to say was, "This train is rigged with explosives no one knew were here until an hour ago!" but he knew the best course was to give President Prescott time to alert Prime Minister Elliott and not bring the princess into the loop unless and until it was absolutely necessary. And if it did become necessary, he knew her husband would be the best source for her to hear it from. So Tuck made his move.

"Well, I don't know about the two of you, but I'm finally beginning to feel as though I may get a good night's sleep," he said and finished his tea.

"Yes, I feel that way too," the princess said, and the three of them rose together and headed rearward toward their compartments.

Tuck smiled when he saw the MI6 officers sitting discreetly in a far corner of the dining car, and he gave them a nod as he and his friends exited the car.

"Would you please join us for breakfast in my compartment tomorrow?" the princess asked Tuck. "We only have two more mornings together, and I so enjoy talking with you."

"I'd like that very much, Mary. Thank you," Tuck said graciously.

"Well, then I will arrange to have it served at 9 o'clock if that is okay with you," the princess said and quickly gave Tuck a light, loving peck on his cheek. "Good night, Tuck," she told him and retreated to her compartment.

"Good night, Mary," Tuck replied and accompanied the captain to his compartment.

"Martin, I have something of great importance to discuss with you privately," he told his friend as calmly as he could.

"I'm all ears, Tuck," the captain replied just as calmly. "What's up?" he asked his longtime friend once he'd closed the door to the compartment.

Tuck turned on the stereo beside his easy chair and

raised the volume to mask their conversation from any hidden listening devices.

"Recent developments have created an emergency," Tuck began cautiously.

"Come on, Tuck. Remember who you're talking to," the captain chided him. "Give it to me in plain English. I can take it."

"All I can tell you is that we've discovered some things, and the shit could hit the fan," Tuck said flatly.

"Who's 'we'? And what 'things' have you discovered?" the captain pressed Tuck.

Tuck hesitated a moment too long, and the captain nailed him for it.

"Oh, bloody hell, Tuck! Spit it out! We've been in battle together for Christ's sake!" the captain told his friend angrily and leaned back in his easy chair.

"The U.S and France have three emissaries aboard besides me," Tuck finally said. "I can tell you they are specialists in safeguarding the people and interests of the U.S. and her allies and have been doing exactly that since we left Shanghai. We've learned that Chinese insurgents are aboard and are probably responsible for an explosive material we discovered earlier today."

"What's the explosive, and where'd you find it?" the captain demanded.

"TATP is impregnated in the sound-deadening

insulation in the sidewalls of the entire train," Tuck explained.

"Mother of Satan? Dear mother of God!" the captain gasped. "You know how unstable that stuff can be. We have to get the princess off this train at the next station!"

"Umm, we need to discuss that too," Tuck mumbled and struggled to find the words.

"There's nothing to discuss!" the captain shot back to his friend. "We'll reach Istanbul in a couple of hours. I can have MI6 arrange to have a flight to London waiting for us."

"We're not stopping until we reach Paris," Tuck said quietly but firmly. "We can't risk tipping off whoever has the detonator for the TATP that we're on to them. President Prescott's in discussions with Prime Minister Elliott and President DuPris as we speak. And we can be sure President Chen has been briefed about the danger by his military. It's also a safe bet President Prescott has advised him the *Dragon* will travel directly to Paris nonstop."

"But we're scheduled to stop in Sarajevo and Zurich," the captain argued. "Won't the murderous cowards be suspicious if we don't?"

"Thus far, they have no reason to think we're on to them, which is good because we're not yet even sure of who they are," Tuck admitted, and he knew he must tell his friend about the Edits, who were also on board. But he agonized over disclosing the full sweep of the danger.

"This is gut-wrenching," the captain said. "Our only hope is to maintain control of the *Dragon* without firing a shot. We simply cannot run the risk of a stray bullet sparking an explosion that could cost every life on board. And we must hope the terrorists feel the same way. How could the Chinese allow this to happen?" the captain wondered aloud.

"Ahhhh, that's the mystery we may never solve," Tuck sighed in exasperation. "I'm certain their chief design engineer, Mr. Li, was unaware the sound-deadening foam in the outer walls contains TATP until we discovered it."

"Who's 'we'?" the captain asked angrily. "Damn it, Tuck, do I have to drag every bit of information out of you, or are you going to talk to me like I have half a brain in my head and can be trusted to do the right thing?"

"Okay … okay," Tuck replied. "The man you know as Monsieur Saint-Pallet is a former Lieutenant Colonel in the French Foreign Legion and is serving as a French undercover agent. He and I were given a tour of the *Dragon* by Mr. Li, the chief design engineer. I believe you and the princess had supper with him on the first night of the trip. Saint-Pallet—whose real name is Alexander Rafael Bellarose—actually discovered the TATP when Mr. Li gave us a close look at the sound-deadening material in the outer walls."

"Well, it's clear their security force can't be trusted," the captain said. "So I presume you haven't shared any of this with them?"

"Correct," Tuck said flatly.

"Can we trust the soldiers on board?" the captain asked hopefully

"We're not sure yet," Tuck told him. "So the answer's no for now."

"Can we at least trust the crew at the controls?" the captain asked hopefully.

"Mr. Li vouches for them," Tuck replied. "That'll have to be sufficient for now."

"Is the former legionnaire one of the other three emissaries your president dispatched, or are the French secretly in on this too?"

"They are," Tuck disclosed, "but only in the interest of ensuring the *Dragon* travels uneventfully within her borders."

"How very French of them!" the captain growled sarcastically. "So who are the other two emissaries? Have Mary and I met them?"

"Well, I don't believe you've met Mr. Omar Keller, whose documents say he's a Swiss sword and cutlery sales representative. The other is going by the name Ariana Marie Russo."

"Oh yes, I've met her. And most every gentleman on board has at least noticed her," the captain said with a slight chuckle. "I thought her story about winning a ticket in a lottery sounded a bit dodgy. So now we know there's you, a Frenchman, a Swiss, and an Italian. It turns out the *Dragon* is 'a rolling United Nations' in more ways than the Chinese may ever know. Is that your entire team for this assignment?"

"There are others waiting for us in Paris," Tuck disclosed.

"Let's pray we reach them," the captain said. "Tuck, I must be a part of this. It's best that the princess not learn of it at this time. But I must insist on helping you and your team get everyone on board to safety."

"I don't think that's a good idea, Marty," Tuck replied cautiously.

"You sure as hell don't think you're going to keep me in my compartment sipping tea!" the captain stood up and nearly shouted.

"I had hoped so," Tuck said with a sigh. "This isn't going to sit well with the queen."

"It's going to go over much more smoothly than news that the train carrying her daughter has been blown to smithereens! She urged Mary not to take this trip in the first place!"

"You have a point there," Tuck conceded. "Okay. You're

in. But we take our orders from the president of the United States. Got that?"

"Roger that, as you Yanks say!" the captain said to signal his deference.

"So now that you've asked for it, there'll be no sleep for you tonight, Captain," Tuck said. "You're going to help me find three Chinese super-soldiers."

"That's fine with me," the captain replied. "But I need to know what they look like."

"So do we," Tuck said simply.

"What?" the captain nearly shouted. "Do you know anything for certain about all this?"

"Getting upset about what we don't know doesn't bring answers, Marty," Tuck replied. "We're damned lucky to have discovered the explosive. And we know there are at least three so-called super-soldiers onboard. We must assume they and the TATP are connected, but to tell you the truth, we aren't even sure of that. To complicate this mess even more, we know the soldiers have super-human strength and can change their physical appearance. Last we knew, they were masquerading as dining room attendants, and one of them went by the name Jin Rai. But that was yesterday. Today, we have to assume all bets are off."

"I don't know what the expression means," the captain said. "But I assume it's not good."

"It means we likely know even less than we think we know," Tuck said.

About that time, Rafe knocked lightly on the door to his sister's compartment then leaned against the opposite wall to give her time to awaken and come to the door. He could see her light come on through his side of the peephole in her door.

"What's up?" she asked softly through the slight opening she made when she finally answered the door.

"I have to talk with you," he said softly. "Come with me to a dining car for a cup of tea or something."

"Can't it wait a few hours?" Madeleine pleaded. "I'm really tired."

"It's urgent," was all Rafe felt comfortable telling his sister in that setting.

"Has someone been injured?" Madeleine asked her brother without naming Noah.

"No, but it's urgent," was all Rafe felt he could say.

Madeleine quickly dressed and accompanied her brother to the closest dining car.

"What do you want to tell me?" she asked as she slid into a corner booth by a window. Rafe raised a hand a few inches off the table to alert his sister that an attendant was approaching them with water. He was quietly thrilled it was Mei Yin, whom he hadn't seen in two days.

"Good evening, Monsieur Saint-Pallet! So nice to see you again," she said formally. "Good evening to you as well, mademoiselle. We are serving only beverages and light snacks at this late hour. What would you like?"

"Hot tea and two cups would be wonderful!" Madeleine said as happily as she could.

"I'll be right back," Mei Yin said and flashed a smile obviously meant for Rafe.

"Looks like you have a fan," his sister said playfully. "I hope she doesn't assume I'm your newest romantic interest."

"Lucky for her, I'm so consumed by what I'm about to tell you," Rafe replied.

"Well then, it must be serious," Madeleine said. "Are you comfortable talking here?"

"We don't have much choice," Rafe said. "We'd attract attention using a platform at this hour. People would wonder why we just don't go to a compartment."

"True," Madeleine said, and paused as Mei Yin returned with the tea.

"Here's your tea," Mei Yin said sweetly. "I've also brought a kettle of white tea in case you might like a lighter brew at this hour. It's so nice to see the two of you. These late-night hours are so quiet. We hardly see any passengers."

"It's good to see you too, Mei Yin," Rafe said sincerely. "I didn't realize you had moved to another shift. But now that I've found you, I wonder if you can tell me whether your co-worker, Jin Rai, has returned to work."

"He has not," the young attendant replied with a wrinkled brow. "We are most worried about him. But I didn't realize passengers had missed him too."

"Well, I only ask because I was approached by a security agent the other morning, who asked if I had seen him recently. He said Jin Rai hadn't reported for two shifts. So I've been a bit worried about the young man."

Mei Yin nervously fussed with the collar of her uniform as she listened, and Rafe was disarmed when he caught a glimpse of slight movement under a small patch of skin on her neck.

"Have you spoken with other passengers about him?" she asked nervously.

"I have." Rafe played along to draw her in and keep her at the table long enough to get a good look at what was happening on her neck. "If you can join us for a few minutes, I'd like to share what I've learned."

"I'd like that," the pretty attendant said. "I'll get a cup and be right back."

"What is this about, Rafael?" Madeleine huffed and let his real name slip when Mei Yin left the table. "I hope you didn't wake me out of a sound sleep and drag me here just to listen to you flirt with an attendant."

"It's important, Sis," Rafe promised. "Trust me … and watch her neck."

Rafe had no problem with Madeleine using his real name. He was quickly becoming so focused on foiling the unseen terrorists that pretense seemed unimportant now.

Before exiting the kitchen, Mei Yin drew a nine-inch filleting knife from a knife block, slipped it under her apron, and carefully tucked it into the waistband of her skirt.

"What about her neck? Why?" was all Madeleine could say before Mei Yin returned to their table and slid into the booth beside her.

"Thank you for the kind invitation," Mei Yin said with a smile. "We would never be allowed to do this on other shifts. But as you can see, we are all alone at this hour. "

"Yes, everyone else is probably sound asleep by now," Madeleine had to say.

"So Monsieur Saint-Pallet, what have you learned about Jin Rae?" she asked intently.

As she and Rafe talked, Madeleine settled back against the wall with her cup in both hands and pretended to focus on her tea while she was actually focused on Mei Yin's neck.

"Well, I may have overstated what I learned," Rafe admitted to buy time. "I did learn that another passenger spoke with Jin Rae, who shared some sensitive information with him and expressed the desire to defect." Rafe thought he'd play a card and see how Mei Yin reacted.

The pretty attendant nervously fidgeted with her collar again, and Madeleine got her first look at the movement Rafe had seen under her skin, caused by involuntary muscle contractions. It was the telltale sign she was an Edit. Madeleine knew her shock at seeing the neck movement was written all over her face. So she was glad Mei Yin was focused on speaking with Rafe, who was sitting directly across from her. As they spoke, Rafe saw his sister's reaction through the corner of his eye, and he knew she was beginning to grasp the seriousness of the situation. But there was much she didn't know, and Rafe intended to address that shortly.

"Do you have any idea what the information was that he shared?" Mei Yin asked.

"Actually, I don't." Rafe lied about the information to see her reaction. "Jin Rae wrote it in a note he passed to the passenger, who gave it to me because he feared having such sensitive information in his possession,"

"What did you do with it?" the young attendant asked with obvious interest.

"I have it in my compartment," Rafe told her, certain that only an Edit would care.

"This is so intriguing!" Mei Yin practically squealed.

"This trip has been so boring until now. I can hardly believe such excitement is finally happening!"

"Would you like to see the note?" Rafe asked, hoping she'd take the bait.

"Oh, could I?" Mei Yin gushed. "I'd love to. This is so exciting!"

Madeleine was unsure of what her brother was up to. But she followed his lead as he and Mei Yin slid out of the booth and headed for his compartment. She suspected there was no note and that her brother had lied to lure the attendant to his compartment. She also knew it wasn't normal for muscles to move as they moved in the attendant's neck. It looked as though something alive was trapped beneath the skin and desperately looking for a way out.

None of this made any sense to Madeleine. But she knew her brother well enough to be sure he was on to something important and potentially dangerous, so she followed them to Rafe's compartment and excused herself to use the bathroom when they arrived. She locked herself in the bathroom and forced her mind into high gear. If she and her brother were in danger, they were stuck without weapons. Her mind raced and then locked on the porcelain commode. She knew the lid was solid wood, and she undid the two plastic screws that held it in place.

"So, where is the note?" Mei Yin abruptly asked once Rafe had closed the door.

"I lied to you to get you here," Rafe confessed. "I didn't want to ask you whether you are an Edit in public."

"Why would you think I'm an Edit?" Mei Yin asked innocently.

"Why would you know what an Edit is unless you are one?" Rafe shot back at her.

"Aaaahhhhhh!" the attendant screamed wildly, pulled the filleting knife from her waistband, and charged at him. "I will cut you so bad you will wish you had never been born!"

Rafe reflexively sidestepped the move, and the Edit flew past him and onto the sofa, which fell backward under the force of her landing. Mei Yin sprang to her feet, lifted the sofa as though it were a folding chair, and tossed it effortlessly across the room. Madeleine bolted out of the bathroom with the wooden lid as Mei Yin leaped onto Rafe, clamped her legs around his torso, grabbed a handful of his hair, and twisted his neck at a painful angle. Madeleine was shocked to see that her brother's strength was no match for the Edit's power. She'd seen enough.

"About face!" she shouted, and Rafe turned just enough to present Mei Yin's back to her.

Madeleine raised the lid high overhead and brought it down with all her might, flat onto the Edit's skull so forcefully the lid split in two. The Edit fell to the floor unconscious.

"Well, now that we know she's dangerous, what do we do with her?" Madeleine asked.

"I didn't think that far ahead," Rafe admitted. "I don't have anything to tie her up with, and you can't keep whacking her over the head."

"I'd sure like to," his sister replied.

Rafe looked about the compartment but saw nothing strong enough to restrain the Edit. Then he glanced at the speed indicator over the door of his compartment.

"Rafe, what are you thinking?" Madeleine asked warily, afraid she knew the answer.

"We're only moving at forty-six kilometers an hour," he told his sister. "That's less than thirty miles an hour … and there's nothing but loosely packed sand outside."

"Rafe, there's a security camera right outside this compartment," she reminded him. "There's another one at each platform exit."

"There are way too many cameras for someone to be watching them in real time," he reasoned. "And by the time they get around to viewing the video, we'll be in Paris, if not London. In the meantime, she'll just be another missing dining car attendant, like Jin Rae."

"Oh, my god!" Madeleine gasped as her gaze returned to the unconscious Edit.

Rafe looked down at the Edit he knew as the young and pretty Mei Yin and literally watched the muscles in her face and entire upper body move with a will of their own and transform the unconscious Edit from a youthful woman to a man in his mid- to late-thirties. It was much the same transformation Tuck had witnessed while Jin Rai slept in his compartment.

"Tuck tried to describe this to me," Rafe told his sister. "Tuck told me about how Jin Rae reverted to his true appearance while he slept. He called himself an Edit and said there were two more aboard with orders to return him to China before he can defect and exposes the Reds ultra-secret super-soldier program. This beast is obviously one of them. Do you really want to tangle with him again when he wakes up?"

Without responding verbally, Madeleine answered her brother by helping to lift the Edit to his feet. Then they lugged him to the nearest platform exit and pushed him off the train.

"One Edit down, two to go!" Rafe said after they heard the muffled thud of the Edit landing on the sand.

14

LONG ODDS IN A DANGEROUS GAME

Q had parked himself on a bench across the street from the hospital's emergency entrance and waited for Genevieve to re-emerge. After a couple of hours on the bench in an increasingly cool Paris night, he began to think he'd made a big mistake. He'd originally thought that quietly introducing himself to her outside the hospital and discreetly asking about Chastain would bring him more answers than flashing his badge and attracting unwanted attention inside the hospital.

Just as he began to seriously second-guess his decision, Genevieve finally exited the sliding doors with a weary look on her face. Part of Q hated to bother her at such a late hour, but he'd waited so long without involving the police he felt entitled to whatever information she had about Chastain. He quietly kept pace with her from across the narrow street, just long enough to put distance between them and the hospital. Fifteen minutes later, he couldn't wait any longer and calmly strode across the street with his U.S. Marshal badge in his hand.

"Pardon me, mademoiselle," Q said calmly. "I'm U.S. Marshal Quinton Marshall. I'm here on official business, and I'm hoping you might be able to provide me with some information about the gentleman you brought to the hospital tonight."

"A U.S. Marshal who wears a Stetson hat," Genevieve pondered the image it conjured. "That makes you a real-life cowboy, doesn't it?" she asked with deepening interest. "What possible interest can a cowboy from the States have in a French ne're-do-well?" she asked. "And what sort of information do you seek? I'm really not at liberty to discuss patients with anyone but their authorized immediate family members and attending medical personnel."

"Before I answer your questions, I first must beg your forgiveness for my obvious lack of decorum in failing to respectfully ask your name," Q said sincerely.

"I'm Dr. Genevieve Valoir," she replied and gave Q her card. "I'm a resident cognitive psychologist at Paris Aide Santé Mentale."

"I'm pleased and honored to meet you, Dr. Valoir," Q said earnestly.

"Oh, please call me Genevieve," she told him with a shake of her head. "Perhaps speaking with you won't feel quite so official and will help me understand what your interest is in my patient. But I must repeat my legal obligation to maintain the confidentiality of his information—what little I know of it."

"Let's begin there," Q said. "Do you know him as Nostradamus or Gabriel Chastain?"

"Well, he introduced himself to me as Nostradamus … and he seems genuinely convinced he is, in fact, the notorious seer of the sixteenth century. He also appears to be completely oblivious to the reality that it's not possible. He once said the name Gabriel when I caught him off guard, but he said he didn't know why it came to mind, and he couldn't recall a last name."

"He's Gabriel Chastain alright," Q assured her. "The man you brought to the hospital tonight is a court-marshaled ex-foreign legionnaire who struggles with a traumatic brain injury and PTSD. He's also France's most decorated living hero. But most important at this moment, he's an escapee from La Santé Prison. Is that complex enough for you?"

"Well, I'm beginning to understand the importance of his being Nostradamus," the pretty psychologist remarked. "What more interesting and adventurous character could one become in the process of walling off such a complex and unfortunate series of life events? And what is your interest in him, marshal? Do you have a warrant for his arrest, or did you travel all the way to France to merely bring him more bad news?"

"I'm in Paris for a totally unrelated purpose and never

dreamed I'd cross paths with Chastain," Q told her. "But a wise man I know always says everything happens for a reason, and I don't believe tonight happened so that I could arrest him or even bring him bad news."

"That's good to hear, Marshal," Genevieve said, "because I feel neither would benefit him in his current state. So what's next?"

"Depends on you and the hospital's policy, I suppose. The police are looking for him," Q assured her. "Frankly, I'm surprised you weren't aware of that when you met him. His mug shot and photo must be on TV day and night."

"I don't watch TV," she replied.

"Yeah, me either," Q told her. "That's why I didn't realize he had escaped until you two walked by me tonight."

"Well, the hospital will have to notify the police the moment they realize he's an escapee," Genevieve said. "Someone at the hospital is bound to recognize him. So if they haven't called the police already, they soon will."

"He checked himself in. Can he check himself out?" Q asked urgently.

"Yes, of course," Genevieve replied. "But visiting hours aren't until 8 a.m."

"Hopefully, they'll make an exception for my badge. What name did he use to check in?" Q asked even more urgently.

"Gabriel Seer," the attractive psychologist told him. "We didn't dare use Nostradamus."

"I'm going to talk with him," Q told her as he hailed a cab. "Do you want a ride home?"

"No, I always walk, thank you," she said with a parting smile and finally headed home.

Q entered the hospital minutes later, showed his badge, and got Chastain's room number.

"Hello, Gabriel," Q said calmly when he entered Chastain's room and found him watching the news on the TV mounted to the wall opposite his bed.

"You look familiar," Chastain said, "but I don't recall your name. And why did you call me Gabriel?"

"It's Q," the marshal said. "Don't you recall the copter ride you gave me in the States?"

"My name is Nostradamus," Chastain said warily. "I've been to the United States. But I've never been in a helicopter, and I certainly don't know how to fly one."

"Maybe *you* don't, but Gabriel Chastain does," Q shot back, "and he's inside of you."

"You're the second person to tell me that tonight," Chastain said. "But I swear I don't know what you're talking about."

"Do you remember escaping from prison two days ago?" Q asked.

"I do, and I recall what it required," Chastain said. "But I don't know why I was there."

"That's because you were locked up as Gabriel Chastain for being AWOL from the foreign legion and for injuring those who tried to capture you while you were Nostradamus," Q explained. "You can't remember being one when you are the other because you sustained a brain injury in an act of heroism as a legionnaire."

"They cannot lock up Nostradamus for things Gabriel Chastain did," Chastain said. "I will not stand for it, and I will make them pay."

"That's what you told them," Q said in a reckless moment of inspiration. "But they didn't listen, and they're looking for you now to lock you back up. They don't understand your value to France in defending against an attack on a train due to arrive here the day after tomorrow."

"What train?" Nostradamus asked with new energy.

"A high-speed train is coming from China with a couple hundred people aboard from around fifteen countries, including France," Q told him.

"Is Legionnaire Alexandre Bellarose on board?" Chastain asked with the spark of a plan.

"He is," Q said and knew Chastain was taking the bait.

"Then I must get out of here now!" Chastain said. "Will you help me?"

Q stuck his head out the window, assessed the surroundings, and smiled.

"We're only on the third floor," he said happily. "And there's nothing below but a dark, deserted alley. We'll be out of here in no time. Wait here; I'll be right back."

Q slipped into the quiet, night-shift hallway, into a closet marked *Linens*, and emerged with an armful of sheets. He hustled back into Chastain's room, and the pair quickly tied a sheet rope and fastened it to the heating radiator beneath the window. Then Q tossed the rope out the window, and the two of them took their turn lowering themselves into the alley and were gone.

Q knew he was playing very long odds in a dangerous game. Chastain was an extremely proficient killer and even more dangerous while Nostradamus. And that's who he had on his hands running out of that Paris alley. He hoped the "spell," or whatever it was that held Chastain captive while he thought he was the French seer, would fade, and the hero legionnaire would reappear as he had in Arizona two years before. But it looked unlikely by the time they reached Q's hotel room.

"I need a shower," Chastain said the moment Q closed and locked the door.

"Be my guest," Q told him. "Bathroom's straight ahead. You'll find everything you need in there. Take your time. And I'll go next."

Q's mind was running at full speed when he heard Chastain turn the shower on. As the delusional Frenchman's rendition of "Alouette" echoed in the bathroom, the U.S. marshal wrestled with what to do with the escapee now that he had him. The fugitive showed no signs of reverting to the heroic Chastain Q had seen once before and needed to see again to justify having helped the ex-legionnaire elude the police and avoid returning to prison.

Q had no doubt Chastain could help the team if the *Dragon* brought violence to Paris. But Nostradamus would surely make things worse. So by the time the seer stepped out of the shower, Q knew what he must do. And the seer never saw it coming.

"I'm sorry," Q said sincerely as Chastain collapsed in a heap when Q clubbed him behind the left ear with his heavy, nickel-plated Colt Python.

The marshal then restlessly waited for Chastain to regain consciousness. He held his breath as Chastain finally sat up nearly an hour later and rubbed the back of his aching head.

"Where am I?" Chastain asked in a fog of confusion.

"Man, oh man, am I ever glad to hear you ask that!" Q said happily. "Welcome back!"

"Q!" Chastain shouted. "Where are we? And where did you come from?"

"Don't get too excited, big guy," Q said. "You're still in

Paris, and you have every cop in the country lookin' to toss you back in the slammer."

"How did I get out?" Chastain asked honestly.

"Your best friend and worst enemy, Nostradamus, made it happen," Q told him.

"How?" Chastain asked plaintively.

"We have time to sort that out," Q replied. "But in the meantime, just know that France and the rest of the free world may soon need your help. And you need to be available. Stay here. I'm going to step out and grab us something to eat. You hungry?"

"I'm starving!" Chastain told him.

"Sit tight," Q said. "I'll be back shortly."

Once Q was outside, he pulled Genevieve's card from his pocket and called her.

"Hello, Dr. Valoir. It's Marshal Marshall," he said quietly. "I have Chastain."

He expected a shrill demand to return her patient. Instead, they had a calm conversation about Chastain's condition and his value to the nation during Q's cab ride to an all-night market.

"God be with you both … and with France," Genevieve said as she ended the call.

15

Q arrived at the market just as the manager decided to clear his sandwich case for next to nothing. So the marshal headed back to the hotel with more sandwiches than he knew what to do with—that is, until his cab stopped in front of his hotel and he found Doc, Jenny, and Louis waiting for him on a broad bench just outside the front doors.

"Howdy, Q!" Jenny said in her best cowgirl imitation.

"Welcome to the City of Light!" Q replied, happy to see the trio again. "I've got plenty of sandwiches, but you'll have to get your own rooms. I already have a guest, and I'm not sharing my bathroom with more than one person."

"Q, you devil!" Louis said demurely.

"What are you talkin' about, Q?" Doc asked in disbelief,

knowing better than to think his best friend had a woman in his room.

"I'm in room 307," Q told them. "After you get registered, come on up, and I'll introduce you all. And bring something to wash these sandwiches down with."

Jenny and Louis hadn't known Q nearly as long as Doc, so his cryptic talk of a "guest" didn't strike them quite the same way it struck Doc. He was thoroughly mystified and a little wary as they stepped off the elevator on the third floor and knocked on Q's door.

"Come on in!" Q loudly invited them in innocently enough. "I said I'd introduce you, but you all have met before," he said and bit into a roast beef sandwich as he led them into his suite.

"Gabriel!" Jenny shouted and threw open her arms. "I feared we'd never see you again!"

"My gosh, man!" Louis said more quietly. "You look terrific. When did you get out?"

"I think the important question is *how* did you get out?" Doc said and hugged Chastain. "You do look good, though," Doc agreed. "Prison certainly hasn't gotten the best of you."

"According to the news, he had help from his old friend and worst enemy," Q told them.

"Nostradamus?" Jenny blurted out, surprised that Chastain was still fighting that battle.

"Bingo!" Q shot back.

Doc took Q aside and quietly explored the particulars.

"So how long ago did he revert to Chastain?" he asked.

"Just about an hour and a half ago when I clubbed him with my Colt," Q said with an uneasy smile. "I hated to do it, and I knew it was a long shot. But we saw him in action in Arizona, and I know we can use his help if things get really sticky when the *Dragon* arrives."

"Perhaps," Doc agreed. "But in the meantime, we're harboring a fugitive. We'd better run this by the president before we all end up in the news."

"I know you're right, Doc," Q admitted. "Just don't tell him I clubbed Chastain, okay?"

"Well, come what may, it appears you did Chastain and everyone else a favor," Doc said. "I'm sure everyone would rather deal with the ex-legionnaire than Nostradamus."

"Are there any questions before I speak with President Prescott?" Doc asked the team.

"What are you all doing in Paris, and where's the rest of the team?" Chastain asked.

"You haven't briefed him?" Doc asked Q in surprise.

"I figured I'd feed him first," Q said. "Then you guys showed up. So now's the time."

"We're on a mission to help ensure a high-speed

Chinese train called the *Dragon* arrives in London safely along with passengers from around the continent, including England's Princess Mary and her husband," Doc said. "Tuck, Noah, and Madeleine boarded the *Dragon* in Shanghai and are helping to protect it and the royal couple. It's scheduled to briefly stop here in Paris in two days, then proceed to a grand reception in London."

"So what's so risky about this train that you all got involved?" Chastain asked.

"The U.S., France, and England believe there are sinister forces hiding among the passengers and crew, who plan to hijack the train and Princess Mary at an opportune moment to force an international incident. And you should know about one other passenger."

"Who's that?" Chastain asked with interest.

"Rafe," Doc said and braced for Chastain's reaction.

"Rafe?" Chastain practically shouted. "I had a dream he was on a train, but the last I heard, he was wandering the back alleys of Marseille after being court-martialed and serving a stretch in the brig."

"We're not in that loop," Doc told him honestly. "But you can be sure that the last thing France wants is for an international incident to happen on its soil. So offhand, I'd say France realized how much they still need him."

Chastain caught Q's eye and led the marshal to the far side of the large room.

"I heard Rafe assaulted an officer for making a crass remark about me," Chastain said. "It hurt to hear that because I deserve ugly remarks. But knowing Rafe like I do, that didn't matter. I'm sure it still doesn't. So I'm grateful France has given him another chance. It's bad enough to live with having screwed up my own life. It would be even worse living with the thought that I was the cause of him screwing up his life. I'm such a mess."

"We're not what happens to us, Gabriel," Q told him. "We're what we do with it. And starting tomorrow, you're going to help us ensure this mission doesn't get screwed up. Got it?"

"Roger that!" Chastain barked back at Q.

"Everyone can get some sleep," Doc called out. "By now, President Prescott's awake. So I'm going to call him to exchange updates. See you in four hours."

"Roger that!" everyone answered him and headed to bed.

As the *Dragon* barreled northwest toward Sarajevo, Noah realized he would soon have to execute the download of the data the U.S. intelligence community had identified as possibly having military applications. He'd just talked with Doc, who told him the president had confirmed the *Dragon's* chief driver was only about an hour away from being informed by People's Liberation Army Lieutenant Colonel Aiguo

Hyang that the train must become an express to Paris—that the planned promotional stops in Sarajevo and Zurich had been canceled due to an outbreak of an aggressive flu virus.

Noah decided that the moment of that announcement, coupled with some attention-grabbing move by his wife, would provide the distractions he needed to make his move on the computer compartment. So he headed straight to the dining cars in the hope that Madeleine would be holding court in one of them. They needed to coordinate a diversion that would free him to access the computers in the forward end of the second car and give him at least ten minutes to download the files onto a miniature flash drive he would then swallow. It was a simple task, really. Even swallowing the tiny flash drive would be almost effortless. The only danger was in being discovered. So he would rely heavily on his wife's ability to attract as much attention as she could for as long as she could.

As they had planned the night before, Madeleine was in the forward-most dining car. Three gentlemen were standing at her table, trying their best to make her laugh while they stole glances at the low neckline of her deep purple sequin dress. The scene both bothered and motivated him. He knew his wife loathed the role she was playing, yet she embraced it because she understood its value to the mission. He likewise understood the sooner he downloaded the top-secret data, the sooner Madeleine would no longer have to serve as the *Dragon's* Mata Hari.

Noah saw the relief in Madeleine's eyes the moment she noticed him approaching.

"Ah, Signore Keller!" she said loudly. "How nice to see you again. I had hoped we would have more time to talk before the end of our trip. Please sit with me a moment."

"Why, thank you, Miss Russo," Noah replied as he slid into the booth beside his wife. "I had also hoped for another opportunity to spend time with you."

Madeleine grasped her husband's upper arm, pulled him close, and whispered in his ear, "Don't we have to get those files soon?" she asked.

"We do," Noah whispered back. "It will help tremendously if you head in the direction of your compartment when you hear the driver announce that we won't be stopping in Sarajevo and Zurich. Then I'll need you to return here about five minutes later, claim that you've been assaulted, and pretend to faint. That, and the announcement, should easily provide the distraction and the time I'll need to access and download the data I'm after without being detected."

"You got it, sweetheart," she said and nibbled his ear for the benefit of the male passengers who were closely watching the two of them carry on like two lovers.

With that, Noah slid out of the booth to free his wife to again monopolize the attention of a good number of men in the car. As Noah paid for a cup of coffee, buttered rye toast and a sweet roll, he saw Rafe and

Tuck enter the dining car from opposite ends as planned. With everyone in position, he ascended the stairs to the observation deck to await the lead driver's announcement. Halfway through his light breakfast, the announcement came over the intercom.

"Good morning, ladies and gentlemen," the lead driver said in his most formal voice. "We have just learned that our scheduled stops at Sarajevo, Bosnia and Herzegovina, and Zurich, Switzerland, have been deleted from our itinerary, and we will now cruise directly into Paris, France with all deliberate speed. We have been informed that a recent outbreak of a particularly aggressive strain of influenza A virus is widespread and causing particularly unpleasant symptoms at both locations and parts in between,

"The good news is that you can rest assured that the *Dragon's* state-of-the-art interior pressurization system and our space-age ventilation and air filtration technologies totally eliminate any possibility of the virus gaining entry to the train as we transit the region. So we will arrive in Paris unaffected by the virus and approximately four hours ahead of schedule."

Noah was pleased by the excited, chaotic reactions of passengers on the observation deck and in the dining area below. So as he sipped the last of his coffee, he took the miniature flash drive from his jacket pocket and descended to the dining level to watch Madeleine exit the car as planned. While she was gone, Noah moved close to the exit his wife had used and where she would soon reappear. He had no doubt she would command the attention of everyone in the dining car. What they were both banking on was that she could cause enough of a scene to capture the attention of everyone between the dining car and the second car of the train, where the computers were located, for at least ten minutes. He knew that was a tall order, but he also knew his wife was an extraordinary woman. So he prepared to act swiftly when Madeleine reappeared. And reappear, she did.

"Help me! Someone help me, please!" Madeleine gasped as she staggered into the dining car with one shoulder of her dress torn and hanging at her side. Blood was trickled from her scalp, and her left eye was nearly swollen shut.

Noah was caught so off-guard by her appearance and performance his instinct nearly kicked in and compelled him to run to her. But he caught himself, remembered it was all an act, and turned and hustled in the direction of the *Dragon's* computers. Twenty minutes earlier, he'd spotted a young security guard hanging out at the forward exit, and he saw the fob hanging from a thin, flimsy chain around the unsuspecting guard's neck. Noah broke into an all-out run. As he approached the exit, he pretended not to see the guard and ran into him so hard they both fell to the floor. As Noah apologized and helped the young man to his feet, he deftly yanked on the chain so hard it snapped like paper. Noah then quickly left the dining car with the fob while the guard was none the wiser. Noah sprinted in the direction of the computers with Tuck and Rafe close behind. Everyone between the computers and dining car ran to see what had happened to the lovely and flirtatious Ms. Ariana Marie Russo.

The double doors to the computer compartment silently opened as Noah approached. He strode into the compartment, and his two teammates stood at a window just outside the doors and talked about the scenery racing by. Six and a half minutes later, when the data download was almost complete, Noah's heart missed a beat because he thought he'd heard a muffled thud. He was sure of it. But the banks of computers were just four feet high, and Noah saw no one else in the small compartment. He listened intently and heard nothing more while the download was completed. But he heard a second thump just as he swallowed the tiny flash drive.

With the files secure inside him, Noah knew he should leave. But he heard another muffled thud and a grunt that seemed to come from locker-style cabinets along the opposite wall, and his curiosity got the best of him. When he opened the first cabinet, the one beside it erupted with grunts and thuds. He threw open the second cabinet door, and a foul-smelling, duct-tape-bound and gagged man fell into his arms. Noah lowered the man to the floor then poked his head out of the compartment.

"I think I've found your missing Edit," he said, and Tuck hustled into the compartment.

"Jin Rai!" Tuck exclaimed when the man rolled over to face him and strained against the tape that bound him. "He looks and smells like he's been in here the whole time," Tuck said and pulled at what appeared to be several rolls of tape wrapped around Jin Rai's wrists and ankles.

"I've got this," Noah told the retired Navy captain and clicked open the same type of nine-inch switchblade he'd given to Rafe. "Why in the hell would someone use so much tape?" he asked as the knife did its job.

"Someone who knows the strength of an Edit," Tuck replied. "Like maybe another Edit."

Tuck knew in that moment Li Wei was the third Edit. Like Jin Rai and Mei Yin, Li Wei was a dining-room attendant. Rafe had caught him in a rage with Mei Yin days earlier, and he'd been scarce since Rafe and Madeleine threw Mei Yin off the train. Two sharp knocks on the compartment doors came next, and Noah quickly opened them.

"We've got company," Rafe said softly and nodded toward Li Wei, who had just entered the far end of the car.

The pair quickly slipped into the computer compartment and hid among the computers with Tuck and Jin Rai. Li Wei went directly to the cabinet where he'd stuffed Jin Rai and was shocked to find it empty.

Noah, who had no idea of the Edit's power, pounced on him from behind and wrapped his arms around the man's shoulders and chest.

"Oh, merde!" Rafe said under his breath and tackled the Edit around the legs, which sent them all crashing to the floor.

Li Wei easily shook both men off him, leaped to his feet, grabbed Tuck by one arm, and shook him like a ragdoll. But Tuck kept his wits about him, planted both feet against a bank of computers, and launched himself and Li Wei hard against a wall. The Edit's head took the brunt of the impact, and he fell to the floor in a heap.

"Nice work for a retired Navy man!" Rafe said half in jest.

"I'm just retired … not helpless!" Tuck barked back, defensively.

"That's good to hear," Rafe told him and lifted Li Wei's upper body off the floor. "Grab his legs and follow me."

"Where are we taking him?" Tuck asked when Rafe told Noah to head out of the compartment.

"He's about to join his partner in crime," Rafe grunted as they struggled with the Edit, whose muscle mass weighed far more than any of them would have guessed.

The four of them squeezed onto the small platform, and Rafe and Tuck held the Edit upright while Noah wrapped both arms around the hulk's thighs and lifted him.

"Wait! Wait!" Rafe shouted. "Check his pockets! He must have the detonator!"

They didn't find it, and the Edit began to awaken as Noah lifted him off the platform again.

"Where's the detonator?" Rafe shouted at their captive.

"What detonator?" the Edit struggled to ask. "I don't know what you're talking about."

"You must!" Rafe shouted angrily and nodded at Noah to lift the Edit again. "Now tell us where it is, or you'll be missing too!"

"You go to hell!" the Edit told him and began to struggle and regain his strength.

"You first!" Rafe shouted and shoved the Edit backward over the railing

The *Dragon* was moving much faster than when Mei Yin left it in a similar fashion. But the trio had no choice.

"Well, it wasn't exactly a smooth operation," Noah sighed and flashed Tuck a weary smile. "But we have the data *and* our defector. So we won't need this anymore," he said happily and tossed the fob to the wind.

"But we still need to find the detonator," Rafe replied. "It wasn't in Mei Yin's quarters. And this guy's not about to blow up a train that's taking him to freedom. So Noah and I will help get Jin Rai to your compartment. Then he and I need to search Li Wei's newly vacated quarters for the detonator. Time for a new face," he told the Edit, and the trio got a close-up look at the incredible transformation.

"There are days I wish I could do that," Rafe said jokingly.

"But think of how much all the mademoiselles would miss your real face," Tuck chuckled as they headed for his compartment.

"You got a point there," Rafe tossed back at him.

"I'll gladly help search for the detonator," Noah said. "But first, I need to check on Madeleine. That was some performance for an amateur, wasn't it?"

"Roger that!" Tuck and Rafe chuckled.

The trio huddled around Jin Rai and escorted him to Tuck's compartment. Then Noah hustled to the infirmary. He knew there was a problem when he saw two armed guards flanking the infirmary door. He figured his best option was to play dumb and say he was checking to see if Miss Russo was alright. One of the stone-faced guards stepped into the infirmary for a moment and returned behind Colonel Hyang.

"Can I ask what your interest is in Miss Russo's condition?" the colonel asked formally.

"I'm just concerned about her," Noah said. "We've become friends during the trip, and I just heard she was assaulted a short while ago."

"That is a most interesting story," the colonel replied with a stern face, "because you can clearly be seen running out of the dining car *after* she appeared and claimed to have been assaulted. I can assure you that she has been thoroughly examined by the physician, and she'll be just fine with rest. But now, I must examine your story just as thoroughly."

The guard who summoned the colonel escorted Noah to his compartment and stood stoically outside the door. Moments later, the colonel walked in, took off his hat, unbuttoned his jacket, and made himself comfortable in an armchair. "I'm prepared to stay here as long as it takes to get honest answers," he said. "So let's begin, shall we? For starters, who are you really?"

"You know who I am." Noah played the only card he had, but the colonel knew better.

"You are no more a cutlery salesman than I am a Hungarian stand-up comedian," the colonel told him gruffly. We *will* find out who you and Miss Russo really are. We will hold you both until we do. So save us all a lot of time and discomfort and tell me who you both are."

Noah's mind was racing as fast as the *Dragon* when the door to his compartment opened, and Rafe and Tuck were pushed in by the second guard Noah had seen outside the infirmary.

"Ahhh, and then there were four," the colonel said sarcastically. "Our surveillance cameras serve us well. And since there's an American among you, I am certain the president of the United States knows who you all are. So now's the time to begin playing fair by letting *me* know who you are. If you do not wish to play fair, I will take the position that you are all Red Z agents and treat you accordingly."

"You do, and you'll live to regret it," Tuck shot back at him.

"So ... anger has arrived," the colonel said with a glint in his eye. "Now, perhaps we can get somewhere. Unless you begin telling me the truth, I am left with only the clues I have. We know Red Z agents are aboard but have not yet revealed themselves. We just assembled the dining room staff, and we are now missing three members. You are clearly not who you pretend to be, which tells me you are not here for the reasons you have declared."

Without so much as a glance at one another, the trio felt relieved that the colonel obviously knew nothing about the flash drive, about the whereabouts of the missing attendants, or the fact that they were Edits. He at least confirmed that Red Z members were on board. But he seemed not to know about the TATP. That clinched it for them. They decided not to give the colonel any information and to try to get all they could from him.

"How do you know Zhēngfú members are aboard?" Tuck asked. "Have you arrested any? Do you know what their intentions are?"

"I am not at liberty to share that information with you," the colonel told him.

"So we are at a stalemate," Tuck replied.

"But you stand on Chinese ground," the colonel said. "So I am in command here."

"Are we under arrest?" Tuck asked flatly.

"Not at this moment," the colonel replied.

Tuck and his teammates turned to leave, but when they opened the door, they found themselves staring down the barrels of the guards' QBZ-95 Bullpup Assault rifles.

"Let them pass," the colonel ordered.

But the guards didn't budge. Red Z had taken over.

"Looks like you're not in command anymore, Colonel," Tuck said flatly.

Despite his bravado, Tuck was convinced things couldn't get any worse. Rafe and Noah were convinced of it as well. But they soon learned they were wrong when the princess, Captain Michaels, and Madeleine were shoved into the compartment at gunpoint.

"I demand to know what's going on!" the princess told

the colonel in a tone so stern it surprised Tuck and his teammates. "Are you the officer in charge?" she asked.

"He was until about ten minutes ago," Tuck sighed. "And I miss him already. It appears the question of whether Zhēngfú plans an assault on the *Dragon* has been answered. And if we aren't already the lead news story around the world, we soon will be."

16

AN ANGEL OF A DIFFERENT SORT

Doc roused Q, Chastain, Louis, and Jenny exactly four hours after he'd dismissed them.

"New plan, folks!" he announced. "The *Dragon's* gone silent and accelerated. China believes it's been hijacked. Beijing has informed Washington and London that they suddenly lost radio contact with the crew and security personnel about the time you hit the sack. Satellite tracking has indicated it picked up more speed than expected just west of Sarajevo. Assuming it's not going to stop in Zurich either, it could reach Paris early tomorrow morning."

"What does the president say about all this?" Q asked. "Who's got the train? Is it the Red Z, the People's Liberation Army, both of them, or some other group entirely?"

"He's not sure just yet," Doc told him. "No one is. So he's pulled out all of our stops. Our team aboard the train's gone silent too. No one's called in, and their phones have been turned off. London can't reach the royals. France has failed to connect with Rafe. We're dead in the water, and the *Dragon* has scrapped its schedule.

"Before the monkey wrench hit the fan, President DuPris had hatched a plan he hoped would catch the terrorists off guard if they commandeered the *Dragon* when it reached Paris. The *Dragon* was going to make an unscheduled stop in Provins, a half-hour southeast of Paris, for an emergency evacuation of the passengers.

"He's already cordoned off a three-square-block perimeter around the station there and ordered a military presence to be in place when the *Dragon* pulls in. But now it's not even clear whether the *Dragon* will stop there or will barrel on through, do the same in Paris, and head straight for London."

"Where's that leave us and the rest of the team?" Q asked, hoping Doc had an answer.

"We're literally all over the map," Doc told him. "Louis, the president wants you and Jenny at the Provins station when the *Dragon* gets there."

"Do you really think it might stop there?" Jenny wondered out loud.

"I don't have a clue," Doc replied with a shake of his head. "But D.C. and London are tracking it real time, and they'll know if the *Dragon* begins to slow down five miles out for a stop at the station. A Chinook 47F chopper will get you two there and will evacuate the royals and our team if the *Dragon* stops. If that doesn't happen, you will hop back on and hightail it back here to Gare du Nort. If the *Dragon* doesn't stop here, we'll know it's going straight to London, and we'll take the chopper across the channel. Technology in the Chunnel will reduce the Dragon's speed to just under 100 miles per hour. That should allow us to arrive in London ahead of it."

"If that bucket of bolts makes it to London, it's going to be a shit show," Q said urgently. "You know MI6 and England's Special Forces Support Group will swarm the station and everything within a several block radius. The British Special Air Service will clear the air space. So what will our roles be?"

"The president was clear, Q," Doc admitted. "We are to do whatever we have to do to save the princess and the *Dragon*."

"Knowing that, I need to get to my weapons lockers," Chastain said.

"Where are they?" Doc asked.

"Stashed not far from here," Chastain told him. "I'll need some help and a truck or van."

"I rented a van while you folks slept," Doc said with a grin. "Follow me."

Back in car seven of the *Dragon,* Rafe's mind was racing through the possible scenarios that might be about to play out. He didn't like the odds of any of them.

"If you're no longer in charge here, who is?" he asked the colonel.

"That's a question for the men with guns outside your door," the colonel sighed.

As if on cue, the door opened, and a hulk of a man in a makeshift uniform with a pearl-handled Colt .45 revolver on his hip and two bandoliers across his chest strode through it flanked by two gunmen carrying QBZ-95s.

"Who the hell are you, and what rock have you been hiding under the whole trip?" Tuck snarled angrily.

"I'm General Wang Yong, supreme commander of the Zhēngfú Legion," the brute replied with an evil grin. "Soon, the whole world will know my name. It's not important where I've been. It's where I'm going that will make the difference to this world. But right now, there is something I need to know."

"There's a whole lot you need to know," the princess shot back defiantly. "And the full force of the United Kingdom will soon teach every bit of it to you."

"Oh, believe me, Princess," Wang Yong said menacingly. "I will be the teacher, and your has-been kingdom will do all the learning. My army and I have no patience or mercy for nations such as yours, content to rule small, remote parts of the globe. The Zhēngfú Legion will soon live out its destiny, and my sacred homeland will have the entire world bowing at its feet."

"You're insane if you believe that!" Tuck shot back at the ersatz general.

"I believe it because I know it to be inevitable," the brute said confidently. "And it is inevitable because of me."

"You are insane!" Tuck defiantly told him.

Tuck's words sent a chill down his own spine. *Does this maniac have the detonator?* he asked himself. In that moment, Rafe and Noah silently asked themselves the same question.

"Here's what I must know right now," the general said and clapped his hands.

The door opened again, and Jin Rae walked into the compartment with a guard's QBZ-95 prodding him between his shoulder blades.

Shit! Tuck thought to himself.

"Who is this, and why did we find him in your compartment?" the general asked.

"I have no idea who he is," Tuck lied with relief that the Red Z leader didn't know who—and what—his men had discovered. "Judging by his uniform, he's likely a dining car attendant."

"Then you should thank me for catching him in your compartment, Captain," the general said suspiciously. "And you should do a better job of securing your belongings."

Then the brute leaned in close to the princess and softly told her, "Make yourself comfortable here with your helpless friends. The attack helicopters following us make it clear your government knows we have you. So I will now make my demands to your government. "

Her husband, Captain Michaels, flew into a rage and grabbed the phony general by his shoulders from behind, and one of the guards used the butt of his assault rifle to knock the Englishman to the floor. The guard raised his rifle, but his commander stopped him mid-swing.

"Leave him!" the brute told the guard. "His fate is sealed along with the rest of them."

As soon as the brute and his henchman left the compartment, Jin Rae sprang into action.

"Gimme a razor, quick!" he told Noah as the *Dragon* rolled toward Provins.

"Our heads are on the chopping block, and you want to shave?" Noah asked in disbelief.

Without a word, Jin Rae snatched the razor from Noah's hand and proceeded to shave himself bald.

While Jin Rae shaved, the brute of a commander strode into the lead car, where the crew was being held at gunpoint by four thugs with assault rifles.

"We're not stopping in France," he told the driver. "And

once we clear the platform at Gare du Nord station, we're pushing on to the Chunnel at maximum speed."

"That's very dangerous," the driver told him. "The tracks weren't laid for 600-plus kilometers per hour. You're risking all the lives on this train at that speed."

"My mission is worth the lives on this train and many more," the terrorist leader sneered back at him. "I want this train at the Chunnel in four hours."

"Push this train beyond the limits of the tracks she's riding, and we are all going to die," the driver warned his captor.

"If you don't meet the schedule I just gave you, *you* will die," the terrorist promised, then exited the lead car to check on the security forces his team had surprised and subdued less than an hour earlier.

"How are our unfortunate adversaries doing?" he mockingly asked a member of his legion standing guard over the dozen security officers they had corralled and bound with twist ties an hour earlier in the security car right behind the lead car.

"They pose no threat," the guard replied confidently.

"It is sad to see that the People's Liberation Army has come to this, is it not?" the terrorist commander said while locking eyes with Colonel Hyang. "How very sad, Colonel, that the troops under your shameful command had become so soft and distracted by the world that they did not see us within their ranks until we stepped out from among them and took control."

"You have struck a low blow for your wicked cause," the colonel said as he stood to face his enemy. "But the traitorous war you have started is far from over. And I promise that you will not win."

"You are either highly courageous or incredibly stupid to predict victory despite being so obviously defeated," the terrorist commander sneered mockingly. "I hope the rest of your troops are not suffering from the same delusion where we also subdued them in the tail end of the *Dragon*."

Seeing a guard signal him from the doorway, the terrorist commander returned to the lead car, stepped up to the control console, and lifted the receiver to the hotline linked to Prime Minister Elliott, French President DuPris, and President Prescott.

"I'm so glad you were all gracious enough to accept my call," the terrorist commander said sarcastically. "I appreciate being spared the task of personally explaining to Her Majesty the Queen that her only child's life depends upon your response to the Zhēngfú Legion."

"Get to the point, General Yong!" the prime minister almost shouted. "What do you want in exchange for surrendering the princess and the *Dragon*?"

"Calm down, Mister Prime Minister," General Yong said in a confident, condescending tone. "It's not good for your health to be so angry over a situation that's beyond your control. Not even the four gentlemen I have hanging by their ankles in the rear of the train, who I assume are MI6 agents, are in a position to be of any help to you. You really should train them better."

"You still haven't told us what it is you want!" French President DuPris said forcefully.

"Think harder," General Yong said sardonically. "The three of you seem to have not even considered the possibility that I already have everything I want."

The remark sent an ice-cold chill through the trio. *What if that is true?* each of them thought silently with an uneasiness that was quickly evolving into panic. *What if extortion is not the goal? What if this terrorist's only goal is terror itself? And if it is, why doesn't he mention the Mother of Satan?*

"There's always something more to want," President Prescott interjected in an effort to keep the terrorist talking. "Great Britain wants Princess Mary and her husband back. The U.S. wants Captain Baird back. France and more than a dozen other nations want their people back. Your nation wants the *Dragon* back. What can we offer you in return? Just name it!"

"The world!" General Yong said with a clenched fist. "I want China to rule the world."

"That world will never exist, General," the prime minister said firmly.

"You underestimate me, Mr. Prime Minister," General Yong said boastfully.

"You underestimate the world," the prime minister responded with confidence.

"We will soon know which of us is right!" General Yong told him and hung up as the *Dragon* raced toward Paris at more than 400 kilometers per hour.

The ruthless commander was pleased by the panic that was setting in among the passengers as he walked through the dining cars. He knew it was clear to everyone that the *Dragon* was no longer traveling as planned. So he strode to the center of each dining car, raised his arms and his voice, and threw fuel on the fire.

"Attention everyone!" he shouted in his gruff voice. "I am General Yong, supreme commander of the Zhēngfú Legion, and I now control the *Dragon*. Remain calm and do as I ask and we will all enjoy the remainder of the journey and arrive in London ahead of schedule. If you have any questions about this change of plans, bring them to me because I am the only one who can answer them."

The dining car fell dead silent until Yong left to make the same announcement at several other points throughout the train. Once the passengers were sure he was gone, they burst into a loud chorus of gasps and frightened chatter. Their initial joy about being a part of history had crashed head-on with the terrifying realization that their journey on the *Dragon* may ultimately come to a gruesome end they never imagined. And they soon began to feel a dark uncertainty about whether the *Dragon* would reach London at all, which is precisely the terror the Red Z commander intended to instill in them.

———

"CLOSE YOUR EYES, DOC," CHASTAIN TOLD THE FORMER Navy SEAL on the way to retrieving Chastain's weapons lockers.

"Isn't this a bit overly dramatic?" Doc asked.

"Not in the least," the ex-legionnaire replied. "Rafe and I have stashed an almost priceless collection of armaments and technologies in several locations. Some are one-of-a-kind. Some are illegal to own. We'll both be more comfortable if you don't know how to get where we're going."

"Roger that!" Doc agreed and reclined his seat as he closed his eyes.

Chastain stopped the van a half-hour later and woke Doc to help him load two lockers.

"Rafe hauled around two lockers very much like this when we were chasing you around the States a couple of years ago," Doc told him. "Do these contain the same sort of weapons?"

"Yes and no," Chastain hedged.

"Which is it?" Doc pressed him.

"Mostly yes," Chastain said cryptically. "But some things have changed since then. And if I don't use them, and you don't see them …"

"We'll both be more comfortable," Doc finished Chastain's sentence for him.

"Roger that!" Chastain said with a belly laugh. "You Yanks have some funny expressions!" he added and laughed some more.

Doc's phone lit up with the presidential seal on the ride back to the hotel.

"What's the latest, Mr. President?" Doc skipped the formalities and asked urgently.

"It's official! The *Dragon's* been hijacked by the Zhēngfú Legion, as they now call themselves," the president said. "I'm in the Situation Room and finally have a live satellite feed of the *Dragon*. It blew through Provins and Paris and has picked up speed on the way to the Chunnel. I just spoke to Q and told him you two will join the team at Charles de Gaul. We have a sector cordoned off, and a Chinook C-47's waiting to get you to London. The chopper will be hovering, so you'll have no trouble finding it. We'll be in touch in the air."

"Roger that, Mr. President!" Doc said as the president ended the call.

"Where to?" was Chastain's simple question.

"De Gaulle! Now!" Doc told him. "The *Dragon* blew through town and is headed to the Chunnel. A chopper at de Gaulle's waiting for us. Step on it!"

"What?" Chastain asked innocently.

"Aller vite!" Doc translated.

"Got it!" Chastain barked back and stomped on the gas pedal. "We're ten minutes away."

"Oh, damn it! Wait a minute!" the president grunted.

"What is it?" Doc asked urgently.

"We can't transport Chastain out of France, especially on a military aircraft," the president explained. "Don't put him on that chopper."

"Well, I'm not going to just dump him at de Gaulle," Doc said. "Besides, he's the best France has, and we can use his help. I'll have the chopper set us both down at the French end of the Chunnel in Peuplingues."

"But you'll be no good to the others in London if you do that," the president protested.

"Roger that, Mr. President," Doc said reluctantly. "But we didn't bring him this far to abandon him now. And like I always say, everything happens for a reason. I've given it more thought, and I do believe there's a chance Red Z will park the *Dragon* in the Chunnel. In which case, it might be helpful to have team members at both ends."

"That's a stretch, and you know it, Doc," the president told the best of his Dozen. "But if it's good enough for you, I'll buy it. Godspeed, my good friend."

ON HIS WAY BACK TO THE LEAD CAR, GENERAL YONG couldn't resist returning to Noah's compartment to poke more fun at the princess. It was just the opportunity Jin Rae had shaved his head for. The Edit had told Noah and the others what he planned to do if the general returned to the compartment alone again. He knew his own newly shaved head would distract the terrorist just long enough for the team to pounce on him and get his gun. And that's what happened.

Rafe, Tuck, Madeleine, Noah, and the royals all sprang at the stunned terrorist and knocked him to the floor. To everyone's surprise, Princess Mary came out of the pile with her hair in a mess and the general's pearl-handled Colt in her right hand.

"Good show, Mary!" her husband hollered gleefully at the sight.

The princess gave the pistol to Rafe, who ordered the general to stand and undress. Tuck pulled out his phone and videoed as Jin Rae began undressing too. When they were down to their boxer shorts, Noah tossed the general's shirt to the Edit, who slipped it on. Everyone but the general laughed when they saw that it—and the general's pants—were baggy on the Edit.

"Okay, let him have it," Jin Rae told Rafe, who knocked Jong out with the Colt.

With the general unconscious in a chair, Jin Rae focused intently on the enemy, and the transformation began before the group's very eyes. Slowly at first, but then with increasing speed, the Edit "became" the general in a process that took the group's breath away.

"Are you getting all this?" Noah whispered to Tuck.

"You bet I am," Tuck assured him. "The president won't believe his eyes."

With the transformation complete, Jin Rae put on the general's boots and bandoliers.

"Hogtie and gag the general and follow me," he said in the general's voice.

Rafe made easy work of restraining the terrorist and dropped him in the bathtub, then fell in behind the group as they left the compartment.

"Follow us!" Jin Rae commanded the two guards outside the door, and they obeyed.

But in their haste, the team left the compartment door wide open. As Jin Rae led the team into the lead car, three guards on routine rounds came to the open door of Noah's compartment and decided to investigate. Just steps inside the door, they heard the commotion their general was making in the bathroom, freed him, and followed him to the lead car.

Jin Rae had just enough time to play a long-shot hunch before the general arrived.

"Hand me the detonator!" he ordered no particular soldier among the eight in the room.

Tuck's knees went weak when a soldier stepped forward and handed Jin Rae the elusive detonator, which was no bigger than a pack of cigarettes. Shocked and surprised as the rest of the team that he was now actually holding the detonator, Jin Rae clasped his hands behind his back and subtly waved it at the team crowded into the room and standing close behind him. Rafe carefully took the tiny detonator from Jin Rae and palmed it.

In that moment, the door to the lead car burst open, and General Yong rushed in with his rescuers. Unfazed by how ridiculous he looked in only his boxer shorts, the general barked orders at his troops, but only the three who had brought him there responded at first. The others stood like statues, dumbfounded by the sight of two identical General Jongs, one dressed, the other almost naked. Rafe took advantage of the confusion, made a break out of the lead car, and sprinted away faster than he ever ran before.

"Let him go!" the real commander ordered the two guards who had started after Rafe. "He cannot go far, and this is almost finished."

The ominous remark began to sink in with the team when they heard what was said next.

"Hand me the detonator!" General Jong ordered solemnly.

"I … I already gave it to him," the guilty guard meekly told his general.

"Give it to me!" the general then commanded Jin Rae.

"I cannot," Jin Rae simply said in a bid to buy Rafe time to hide it far away.

"I said give it to me!" the general said angrily.

"And I said I cannot because I no longer have it," Jin Rae said slowly.

In that moment, the general realized the Rafe must have it and flew into a rage.

"Kill this dog!" he screamed.

Tuck's experienced ear heard the click of a safety being released and reflexively took a swing at a guard who was drawing his QSZ-92 pistol in response to the general's command. Tuck's swing knocked the semi-automatic from the guard's hand at the very moment the *Dragon* raced into the Chunnel and plunged the lead car into near-total darkness. As Tuck dove for the QSZ-92, more guards drew their weapons and fired more in panic than obedience. Instinctively, Captain Michaels wrapped himself around his wife as a human shield, and the team wrestled with the guards as the *Dragon's* auto-response lighting suddenly came on.

"Stop!" the general shouted. "Kill the next one who

moves!" he commanded his men with a deadly seriousness, and the team froze when the guards all cocked their QBZ-95s.

"Stop the *Dragon!*" General Jong commanded. "It is over," he then said quietly as the driver brought the *Dragon* to rest about five miles inside the tunnel.

Doc had his satellite phone in his hand when it vibrated, and the presidential seal appeared on the screen.

"Ready, Mr. President," he said simply and switched on the speakerphone.

"You were right, Doc," President Prescott said. "The *Dragon* would be out of the Chunnel by now if it were coming. We've heard nothing from General Jong. He's made no demands, and it doesn't look good. In fact, it's beginning to look like this century's 9/11."

"The chopper's about to put down at the French entrance, Mr. President," Doc replied. "I'm getting off with Chastain, as planned. I'm sending the rest of the team across to the English entrance, and we'll await your orders."

"Nobody is to set foot in that tunnel until we know more, Doc," the president said firmly. "Prime Minister Elliott and President DuPris are patched in on this line, and we'll continue trying to contact the general and the team members he has in there with him. Stay handy. Talk to you shortly," the president said and ended the call.

"Drag a locker off with you!" Chastain yelled to Doc over the rotor noise blasting through the Chinook's open rear hatch as the chopper touched down. "Grab this one," he added. "It's lighter. And whatever you do, don't drop it."

As the *Dragon* came to a halt, Rafe dodged the crush of panicked passengers to make his way through the rear-most dining car. Another car or two farther along, he realized he wasn't being chased by any of the general's men. It didn't make sense in that moment. But it soon would. He stopped for a moment to catch his breath and tried to make sense of the situation. Gulping air with his hands on his knees, he felt the detonator in his pocket begin to get warm. He took it out of his pocket and watched the digital clock slowly wind down to zero, but nothing happened. However, the phone continued to get warmer. Rafe stared at the blank screen for about ten seconds before a new countdown clock appeared with fifteen minutes on it and a banner that read *Auto-Detonate Engaging.*

"Mon dieu!" Rafe said out loud when he realized that he was holding the final link in what he had earlier called the enemy's fail-safe killing machine.

The ex-legionnaire instantly understood that the guard who thought he was handing the detonator over to his leader when he gave it to Jin Rae must have activated an interim countdown clock that gave the holder a few minutes to deactivate the detonator. That could only mean the detonator was a "dead man switch" that would automatically explode with enough force to trigger the Mother of Satan and destroy the *Dragon* and its passengers—and do the unimaginable to the Chunnel—unless the Auto-Detonate mode was canceled during the interim countdown.

Rafe instantly knew he had to get the detonator out of range of the *Dragon*. His only hope of doing that was to reach the rear lead car and, by some miracle, get the detonator out of the Chunnel in less than fourteen minutes.

As Rafe ran for the rear lead car of the train, Chastain already had both weapons lockers open and snapped two mini-jet engines onto a six-foot carbon-fiber delta wing, far beyond the wing Doc had seen Rafe use in Arizona two years earlier.

"Put this harness on," Chastain told Doc and, without looking away from his rigging, held a handful of harness out to Doc.

"The president said not to set foot in the tunnel," Doc reminded Chastain.

"We'll never touch the ground," Chastain replied with a sly smile as he strapped himself to the delta wing and started the engines. "Get that harness on. I only have twenty minutes of fuel."

"What'll we do when we get to the *Dragon?*" Doc asked without an idea of his own.

"We'll figure it out when we get there," Chastain said. "Aren't you the guy who always says everything happens for a reason?"

With that, Chastain took Doc by the shoulders, spun him around to face away from him, and snapped the former Secret Service agent tight against his chest.

"Here we go!" he shouted as the jet engines roared to life, and they left the ground. "Try not to shift your weight or cry!" he shouted to Doc as they picked up speed and headed for the tunnel at more than eighty miles an hour.

RAFE BREATHLESSLY BURST INTO THE REAR LEAD CAR AND was greeted by two guards who were waiting for him with their rifles ready.

"Back off!" Rafe shouted at them and held the detonator up with the bright red countdown clock in their faces. "Open the hatch and let me out, and we all live," he told them, not at all sure if it was true. "You don't have to die for that madman with a death wish," Rafe said. "Open the hatch, and I'll take this detonator as far away as I can in the five minutes left."

Buoyed by the look of indecision on the guards' faces, a young crew member slammed a hand down on the hatch release button, and the hatch sprang open with a rasp of hydraulics. Rafe couldn't believe his eyes when he scrambled out onto the nose of the *Dragon* and saw the delta wing approaching at nearly 100 miles an hour with Chastain and Doc strapped to it.

Chastain gave Rafe a huge smile and saluted him.

"Thanks for everything, my good friend!" Chastain shouted to Rafe as Doc reached for the detonator the ex-legionnaire held out to them. But Chastain quickly maneuvered over the open hatch and pulled the harness release ring as he took the detonator from Rafe. Doc dropped to safety in the lead car with Rafe right behind him. They both stood up just in time to see Chastain fly out of the tunnel and then rocket straight up.

Doc seized that moment and sprang into action while the guards still stared open-mouthed in the direction Chastain had flown out of the tunnel. He kicked a rifle from a guard's hands, and Rafe did the same to the other. Neither guard was any good at hand-to-hand combat, and both were unconscious before they knew what—or who—had hit them.

"How do we put this thing in reverse and pull it out of here?" Doc asked as he shouldered his way through the crew and surveyed the control panel.

"Watch me," a crew member said simply and flipped a toggle switch. "When you're ready to go, just push this throttle stick forward," he added.

"How do we keep the other lead car from overriding us?" Doc asked urgently.

"They can't," the crew member said. "The *Dragon* moves in only one direction at a time."

Hearing that good news, Doc jammed the throttle forward, and the *Dragon* suddenly sprang back to life and headed backward, out of the tunnel. He hoped the sudden jolt would throw the general and his troops in the other lead car off balance and give his team members just enough of an advantage to get the upper hand. It worked. Before the *Dragon* had moved fifty feet, Noah, Tuck, and Madeleine subdued the general and his troops with their own weapons. The cheers of overjoyed passengers echoed through the *Dragon* when they realized they were heading back out of the Chunnel and felt the rush that came with their first hope of freedom.

Meanwhile, the crew of the topsail schooner, *ETOILE*, watched in a jumble of amazement and terror as Chastain rocketed over their vessel and several miles out over the English Channel and soared to more than a half-mile in the air before the detonator exploded and sent the ex-legionnaire hurling toward Earth in flames.

No one on board the *Dragon* saw Chastain's last act of heroism. Not the passengers, who were frantically placing calls to loved ones, and certainly not the members of Doc's team who were preoccupied with the hapless terrorists who spent the ride out of the tunnel on their knees with their hands in the air.

Q, Louis, and Jenny could only see what appeared to them to be a trail of black smoke arching down into the channel. They had no idea they'd witnessed Chastain's heroic end until Doc called Q with what he'd heard from the president about the *ETOILE* crew's account.

Hours later, at a quiet café outside of Calais, after the team had debriefed and decompressed along with Princess Royal Mary and her husband, Captain Michaels, Q once again pulled the card of Dr. Genevieve Valoir from his pocket and dialed her number and flipped on his speakerphone.

The psychologist listened intently to everyone's input of how Chastain's selfless valor had helped save Britain's princess, the *Dragon,* and all the innocent lives on board. Then she fought back tears and told them of the last meaningful conversation she'd had with the ex-legionnaire. She told them about his troubled self-assessment that he was no angel and about his innocent relief at hearing her personal and professional assurance that all men are quite capable of being angels in the best and worst of times, and that she had a good feeling about him.

"I know how much of an angel he was," she said and wiped at the tears on her cheeks. "He was an angel of a different sort, for sure ... but an angel nonetheless!"

EPILOGUE

A lot transpired in the days and weeks following the mission. Doc and Q personally escorted Jin Rae to a White House meeting, at which the president personally thanked him on behalf of the American people for his role in helping to save Britain's Princess Mary and the *Dragon*. The president pledged his full support of Jin Rae's defection efforts and assured him he would closely follow his progress and interactions with the nation's top intelligence agencies.

Rafe underwent a long-overdue reckoning with the demons and resentments that had held such a firm grip on his heart and mind before he returned to Orange-Caritat Air Base, where Commandant Yves Laurent welcomed him back with reinstatement in the legion, complete with a citation, a promotion, and full back pay.

Tuck kept his promise to have Father Patterson back over to his house to finish that bottle of Remy Martin Louis VIII cognac and to continue their conversation about the retired Navy captain's faith and God's faithfulness.

The President's Dozen retreated to Montana once again, where their neighbors had no idea what they did while away. That's what Doc and his team liked most about life around Flathead Lake. It reminded them of how precious the simple life is ... and of the importance of what they did to help keep it that way.

Not surprisingly, it was Madeleine who came away from the mission with the deepest perspective on all that had transpired and the many characters involved. After a few days back home, while sitting in a porch swing with Noah, she jotted a Max Planck quote in her journal so she could easily refer to it in the years and missions to come.

"SCIENCE CANNOT SOLVE THE ULTIMATE MYSTERY OF NATURE. And that's because, in the last analysis, we are a part of the mystery we are trying to solve."

WITH DEEP RESPECT AND GRATITUDE, PRESIDENT Prescott, Prime Minister Elliott, President DuPris, and President Chen arranged for Chastain to be laid to rest beneath a glorious forty-foot European hornbeam tree in the Suresnes American Cemetery with a view of the Eiffel Tower and a simple marker that read:

Rest In Peace
Legionnaire 1e Classe
Gabriel Chastain
An Angel of a Different Sort

Made in the USA
Middletown, DE
23 July 2022

69921974R00166